BRISKWOOD BLOOD RAIN

A NOVEL

CHRISTOPHER JOUBERT

This is a work of fiction. Names of characters, places, and incidents either are the product of the author's imagination or are used fictitiously. Any resemblance to actual persons, living or dead, events, or locales is entirely coincidental.

ISBN 978-0-692-19093-7
ISBN 978-0-692-19094-4

FOR MY PARENTS AND SISTER

IT ALL STARTED WITH A RAINDROP

CHAPTER 1

I stare at the ceiling fan, letting the blades hypnotize me until my eyes flutter shut. The sheets on my bed entangle me like a snake constricting its prey as I twist and turn on my mattress, trying to savor every last second that remains of the nighttime.

Unfortunately, sleep never returns and instead, I end up lost in my own thoughts, which are plagued by a serial killer from a film that I shouldn't have stayed up and watched last night. A branch scratches up against my window, creating a screeching noise that makes the hairs on the back of my neck stand up.

Minutes, possibly hours, later, a clap of thunder shakes me out of my daze. I turn my head to look at the neon numbers that glare menacingly at me from the clock on my nightstand. Somehow, even though I never fell back asleep, I'm running late and the rain definitely won't help. It looks like my first accomplishment of the day will be to book myself a one-way-ticket to detention.

Senior year has kicked my ass. Lately, I just haven't been able to get enough sleep because of the never-ending stream of unnecessary activities that come along with the last year of school. Yesterday, I was forced to take what felt like a million pictures for my graduation invitations. Surprisingly, when I flick on my lamp, I find that my eyes have recovered from the lightning strikes disguised as camera flashes. I stretch and yawn just as the aroma of bacon wafts up the stairs into my room and gives me the extra push I need to begin another day.

"Miles, you're going to be late," Mom shouts from downstairs.

"Mom, you should be used to this by now," I yell back, and my voice echoes down the halls of our large house. I drag myself from the sanctuary of my bed and into the bathroom to brush my teeth. The morning light breaks through the dark storm clouds outside and shines through the window, casting eerie shadows around the bathroom. As I throw on a wrinkled Breaking Bad T-shirt and a pair of jeans splattered with spots of pizza sauce, it thunders again. Actually, that could've just been my stomach growling. I'm not one hundred percent sure. I slam the door and bound down the winding spiral staircase.

When I enter the kitchen, I find Mom dancing to music from whatever decade used an excessive amount of horns. Not stopping to figure it out, I say "good morning" to her over the noise of the blaring portable speaker, grab a handful of bacon, and head toward the front door. She clears her throat behind me, loud enough to be heard over the blasting saxophones and trumpets.

"What?" I whip around and peek my head back inside the kitchen.

"Are you forgetting what I asked you to do last night?" Mom asks. Damn. I honestly have no idea what she's talking about and I don't exactly have the time to listen to her lecture me if I admit that. She glares at me, giving me the thorny and disapproving look that blooms inside of every mom when her child starts to mature—quite terribly in my case. Small wrinkles line the sides of her sad, brown eyes. Her auburn hair is twisted into two braids and peppered with streaks of gray.

Ever since my dad dumped us and moved to Florida with his mistress last year, she's depended on me for every little thing. The sudden betrayal by the love of her life shook her to her core. For two months, she was too emotionally damaged to even leave the house. My grandparents had to help us pay for the bills during that time. After that, she returned back to work as a nurse at the Briskwood General Hospital, where she usually only gets one or two off days.

"Sure, sure, I'll do it after I get out of school. I'm running super late right now. Bye Mom, I love you." I kiss her cheek and run full speed toward the front door. I *really* don't want to go to detention today. I've been a regular there since this year started, but I would still prefer to be bored in my room at home, not at school.

"See you tonight, sweetie. I should be getting home from work right after you. Don't forget to grab an umbrella. It's supposed to ra—" The door closes behind me before she can finish her sentence.

Summers in Briskwood are always unbearably hot. Even though summer hasn't even officially started yet, temperatures have already broken records. The Texas heat smacks me across the face the moment I step outside, and I'm sweating before I even reach my car.

Last year, my grandparents bought me a brand new red Mustang after my ancient truck finally broke down beyond repair. (They're totally loaded, my grandfather is high up on the board of some military research program about four hundred miles south of here.) I unlock my car and leap into the driver's seat.

As I back out of the driveway, a weather report interrupts some terrible song about cheerleaders. The local meteorologist rambles on about a severe thunderstorm that's supposed to roll in later tonight. Briskwood is notorious for its unpredictable weather; the news report is wrong ninety-nine percent of the time. Since the rain is about to come any minute now, it obviously won't wait until tonight. I change the station.

The auto-tuned voice of Blizzy Kelly, a new pop sensation from New Zealand, fills the car. I always find myself speeding to the pulsating beat of this song, which is usually a problem, but today I'm thankful for it. Ten minutes until the tardy bell rings and I'm fifteen minutes away from the school. With Blizzy's help, I can probably make it there in five. I step on the gas and blaze onto the freeway.

The traffic on the freeway robs me of some valuable time. Ten minutes later, I skid into the senior parking lot, throw the car into park, and run toward the building: Briskwood High School, home of the Ocelots. It's a pretty small school, with only five hundred students. Briskwood is right outside the massive city of Houston, but it's not very large at all, with a population of only twelve thousand.

As I go up the stairs to the front door with other stragglers like myself, the tardy bell rings. The loud *clang! clang!* from the bell sends everyone scrambling like ants, but it's too late. There's a popular rumor that the teachers at Briskwood High get bonuses on their salaries for sending as many students to detention as possible.

"Too late guys, another day, another prison sentence," I yell to the fleeing crowd, which warrants a few over the shoulder glares. As the crowd thins out, I head toward my first period class, AP Literature. The teacher, Mr. Panderson, is a special kind of evil. I'm convinced that his life goal is to make as many students as miserable as he possibly can.

Mr. Panderson has a desk set up outside of his room, where he sits for ten minutes at the beginning of class to write tardy slips for the late students. I step into the line of students that await punishment, behind Trevor Johnson, my best friend since elementary school. We met on the playground in fourth grade when a wasp stung me on the arm and one of the teachers asked him to walk me to the nurse. We've pretty much been inseparable ever since. Trevor and I have a lot in common, including the same birthday and the same job. I started at the local theater during my sophomore year and was able to get Trevor on last summer. Apparently, another thing that we have in common is being unable to make it to class on time every single day for the past month.

"Dude, we're screwed. Panda's even more pissed than usual for some reason. He gave Emma a week of detention for not saying 'thank you' when he handed her the slip," Trevor mumbles to me as he steps up to Mr. Panderson's throne of terror.

"Johnson, this is the third day in a row that you've been late to my class. You obviously don't value my time, so why should I value yours? I summon you to four days of educational detainment." A low, sinister laugh rolls out of Mr. Panderson. The desk creaks as his bulging stomach responds to his pleasure of Trevor's misfortune. Trevor thanks the teacher as he's handed the detention paper and stumbles into the silent classroom. He slides into his desk at the back of the room.

"Last but not least, it's Johnson's partner in crime. How are you today, Mr. Parker? I suddenly feel a little generous, so it's only two days of punishment for you. Now, get inside. I have a job to do," he snaps. I walk into the classroom as Panderson lets out another maniacal laugh. Seriously, what is this guy's problem? He enjoys dishing out punishments more than actually educating us—and he isn't subtle about it.

I take my seat beside Trevor, who doodles a disturbing sketch that involves Mr. Panderson and a very sharp stick of bamboo. Trevor can be a little extreme sometimes, but I can't say that I blame him after the stunt that man just pulled.

Panderson waddles his stumpy little body into the room and slams the door, which causes everyone in the class to jump. "Ten students late today. That's a new record. What a shame! Well, the fun is just getting started. Clear your desks. You have a pop quiz over the first three acts of *Hamlet*."

The class lets out a groan that's more unified than the school's choir. Panderson sashays to the front of the room and snatches up a stack of papers from the pile on his desk. I swear his creepy smile grows ten times bigger when he sees the looks of disappointment on everyone's faces as he goes down the aisles to pass out the quizzes.

I can't believe how badly today has gone so far. Between working and waiting until the last minute to do other assignments, I've had zero time to prepare for one of Panda's spur-of-the-moment pop quizzes. I'm so tempted to trip the man as he walks by my desk and gives me a condescending smile that reveals his uneven, coffee-stained teeth.

The quiz might as well be in another language. I circle the first answers that stand out to me and finish way before everyone else, including Trevor, who is focused on drawing another bamboo filled picture on the bottom of his quiz. I pick up my pencil and change a few answers until the teacher bangs on his desk with a yardstick and demands that everyone pass their papers forward. Trevor quickly flips over his pencil to erase the graphic picture on the bottom of his page.

"Johnson, I said pass the quiz forward right now. You should have studied more," Panderson yells.

"Yes sir, I was just, um, correcting one of my answers. *Macbeth* is actually one of my favorite novels," Trevor manages to stutter. He isn't thinking clearly today. I don't know why he thought it would be a good idea to draw an incredibly offensive picture on the bottom of a paper that he has to turn in.

"First of all, we are reading *Hamlet*, a famous play. Secondly, I didn't ask for your opinion on the required reading for my class. Of course a lot of people like it since it's one of the most popular works of literature of all time. Now, pass the paper forward before I assign you to another day of detention." Panderson shakes with rage as he explodes on my friend. The teacher is known for his tirades toward students that don't do exactly what he says to do as soon as he says it.

At the beginning of the year, a cell phone rang while he wrote notes on the dry-erase board and he transformed from his regular scary self into an army drill sergeant. He whipped around to face the terrified students.

"Whose cellular device was that? I'm only going to ask once," his stone-cold voice filled the still classroom. No one answered. He forced every person in the class to give up their phones until the end of the period. If someone refused or tried to say they didn't have their phone with them, he assigned a five-page essay to be completed while going to detention every day after school.

The whole class looks at Trevor, who is now as red as a tomato. His hands tremble when he passes the quiz forward, complete with the only partially erased bamboo art. Sandra McMann, the girl who sits in front of Trevor, lets out a hysterical giggle when she sees what he drew on the paper.

"McMann! Is something fu—"

The teacher tries to begin another rant, but is interrupted. Suddenly, a violent clap of thunder shakes the whole room and we plunge into darkness.

CHAPTER 2

It's so dark outside from the storm that no sunlight comes in through the window. After five minutes of sitting in blackness, with only cell phones illuminating the room, the lights flicker back on. Slowly at first, and then exploding into brightness. People blink the tears from their eyes and look around, dazed and confused. I probably should've heeded my mother's warning to grab an umbrella. I'm going to get drenched when I have to go outside to my next class.

In the short amount of time that the lights were off, Mr. Panderson has fallen asleep in his chair. Screaming and yelling non-stop must use up a ton of energy. Drool spills from his open mouth and moistens the top of his pale yellow button-down shirt. So much for responsible adult supervision. The rest of the class is much more relaxed now that the dictator's presence isn't dominating the room. Everyone separates into their little groups and scroll through their phones while discussing gossip that will be irrelevant a day from now. I turn to Trevor and find that he's returned to his regular light brown color after being publicly humiliated.

"Oh look, you're not a ripened tomato anymore. Are you okay? For a second, I thought you were going to burst into tears. It was that bad," I whisper to my friend.

Trevor flushes again and scowls at me. "Don't act like you haven't had your fair share of public embarrassment. Should we discuss the spaghetti incident from sophomore year?"

Before we can revisit one of the most mortifying events of my entire life, the intercom clicks on and the chipper voice of Principal Petunia Blackwater fills the room. "Good morning, students of Briskwood High. As you may have noticed, unless you were asleep, there was a power outage about ten minutes ago," Blackwater laughs uncontrollably, as if she has just made the funniest, most original joke ever.

Everyone in the classroom pays close attention now. Usually, the principal only talks over the intercom when something very important is about to happen. "Due to the severe weather that is approaching our area, the school district has decided that it is best for everyone's safety if we cancel classes for the remainder of the day. I know that some of you are crushed by this, but I'm sure you'll survive." The entire room erupts into cheers, except for Mr. Panderson, who is somehow still asleep through all of the noise.

"Everyone, please remain in your classes until I come back on to inform you when the buses have arrived to carry out the dismissal," she says, and then the intercom clicks off. The class goes back to talking in their cliques, now with more enthusiasm after receiving this unexpected good news.

Sandra turns around, still fascinated by Trevor's artwork, and hands it to him so that he can finish erasing it from existence. "Trevor, this storm has literally saved you from spending the rest of senior year in detention. Do you have any idea what Mr. Panderson would have done if he had seen this? You have a sick mind."

Trevor grins and plasters an innocent look on his face. He's had a thing for Sandra ever since she moved here from Wisconsin last year. "He made me angry and that was the first thing that popped into my head. I promise I'm not psychotic...unless you want me to be," he winks at her, which triggers another fit of giggles.

"You have to work on flirting. It's almost as bad as your art," she winks back and flashes him a smile that makes the deep dimples on her cheeks pop out. When she turns back around, she makes sure to brush her long blonde curls over the top of his hand. He turns to me, still grinning.

"You're really not on a roll today and it's only first period. Good thing that storm is coming in. Maybe you can rebuild some of your dignity and try again tomorrow." I say, not giving him the approval that he so desperately desires.

"Whatever. You talk like you're Supernova or something. I'm going to the restroom."

"I think you mean Casa—"

Trevor is already out of his seat and headed to the teacher's desk to ask for permission to leave the room before I can correct his mistake. I guess he doesn't realize that Mr. Panderson is still unconscious and wouldn't even notice if he left.

When Trevor reaches the desk, he abruptly freezes. He begins talking to Mr. Panderson and touches the man's shoulder when he still doesn't wake up. The chair that he sits in creaks as his limp body falls to the floor. Trevor shrieks as the whole class turns to the front of the room, realizing that they may shortly have a new story to spread like wildfire around the school. A few people gasp when they see the teacher sprawled out on the floor.

"Don't just stand there. Try to help him!" Sandra screams in a shrill voice.

Trevor kneels down and touches two shaky fingers to Mr. Panderson's flabby neck. After a few long, silent seconds, he spins around. "There's no pulse. He's gone." His voice quivers as he announces to the class that our teacher has died right there in front of us.

A chill runs up my spine when Trevor confirms the death. This is my first time ever seeing a dead body in person. The room falls into silence as everyone takes a moment to process what happened. Nobody moves for at least ten seconds as our brains catch up to the scene that has just played out.

"Ding-dong! The dick is dead!" A sadistically cheerful voice from the back of the room pierces the brief moment of silence. Most of the students in the classroom peel their eyes away from the body to turn around and see who would make such a disrespectful remark at a time like this.

Caston Wells is known for his insensitive comments, but this is a new low. Back in freshman year, Caston's mom died in a plane crash on her way to a business convention. He hasn't been the same ever since. He went from being an all-A student, to getting suspended at least once a month. Over the years, his outbursts have gotten progressively worse and he's completely alienated himself from everyone around him. We always end up in detention together, so I'm familiar with his ridiculous antics.

"Yo, he's been dead for all of five minutes and you're already making jokes? This isn't funny," I shout back at him, my voice shaking a little more than I want it to.

"Who cares? He was a terrible person and deserved what he got. I just had the balls to say what y'all were thinking," he snarls, puts his headphones back on, and goes back to wallowing in his misery.

I clamber out of my seat, and go to where Trevor kneels down, still frozen in place above the teacher's body. "Let's go and see if we can find the nurse or something. There's nothing we can do for him right here." I pull my friend toward the door and we leave the room of traumatized students. No one follows us.

Trevor snaps out of his trance the instant we enter the hallway and rapidly fires off a series of questions. "What do you think happened to him? Do you think I killed him? Maybe he was still alive and hit his head when he fell after I touched him. Am I gonna go to jail? Oh man, I can't go to jail," he says in a winded voice, out of breath by the time he finishes having his meltdown. This is just like Mr. Panderson, ruining someone's day even after his death.

"Trevor, chill. I'm sure that his heart just gave out or something. Maybe that loud thunder gave him a heart attack. I'm sure he was under a ton of stress. I mean, I don't think I ever heard the man talk below a yell," I say in an attempt to calm him down.

"What's Caston's deal anyway? That comment back there was one of his worst ever. I know I have my moments, but that was so out of line. How is that the first thing that pops into your head when a dead person, no matter how much none of us liked him, is laid out in front of you?" Trevor continues, translating his fear into anger.

"Something traumatic like what happened to him can really mess a person up. Still though, he seriously needs to consider getting some help," I say. We fall into a hush as we approach the front office.

I turn the knob to enter the office, just as Principal Blackwater gets back on the intercom to announce that the short school day is over. "Students, the buses have arrived. You may now exit your classrooms and go to the front of the building. If you drive, get to your vehicle immediately and clear the parking lot. Enjoy your day off, and see you all bright and early tomorrow morning," Principal Blackwater's voice echoes into the office from the hallway, which is already beginning to fill with eager bodies anxious to leave school this early.

We walk over to where Ms. Zavalla, the secretary, types on her computer. Words fill the screen as her ring-clad fingers fly across the keyboard. She must be trying to get out of here as soon as possible too. "You're not supposed to be in here. Go home, school's out." She glances up at us for a second and then goes back to her work. Little does she know, her day is about to get a whole lot stranger when she finds out why we've come to the office.

"Excuse me, we need to speak to the nurse and Principal Blackwater immediately. It's an emergency," I say.

"What kind of an emergency?" The unsmiling old woman doesn't even look away from what she types on her computer screen. Her desk is lined with "secretary of the year" awards dating back all the way to 1972. She's been at Briskwood High for a long time.

"It's our teacher, Mr. Panderson. He's dead." I manage to choke out. The disturbing scene constantly repeats in my head. This is affecting me more than I realized.

As soon as the words leave my mouth, Ms. Zavalla stops typing and her tan face pales. Without another word, she leaps from her seat and speed walks to the back of the office. She moves shockingly fast for an elderly lady. A few seconds later, she returns with the nurse and Principal Blackwater.

"What's this I'm being told about a deceased teacher? I'm praying that Nellie heard you wrong. After all, her hearing *has* gotten progressively worse over the years," Principal Blackwater shrieks. Ms. Zavalla gives the principal a look that could cause the second death in the building today.

"You heard her right. It's Mr. Panderson. He died in the classroom when the lights went out. We think the thunder might have given him a heart attack or something," Trevor says, lowering his head as we leave the office and walk back in the direction of the classroom. The nurse nervously twirls his stethoscope as we head toward what is surely one of his most eventful days on the job.

"I went up to him to ask for permission to use the restroom and I thought he was just asleep. When he didn't respond, I checked his pulse and that's when I knew he was..." Trevor's voice tapers off as he explains what happened.

"Miles, do you have anything to add to this?" Principal Blackwater raises a thin eyebrow. Wow, she still remembers my name. When I first started high school, I was bullied for the first few months. My slender body frame, braces, and red hair that stuck up in all directions transformed me into a human target the instant I stepped into the new school. I felt like an imaginary sign that read 'BULLY ME! BULLY ME!' in big, flashing letters hung over my head. The numerous incidents that happened between my tormentors and I landed me in the principal's office many times. After awhile, it was time to get my braces removed and I decided to join a gym. I trained and trained until I fully redefined myself. As my muscles and self-confidence both grew, the bullying slowly stopped and life moved on.

"No, ma'am, I'm pretty sure Trevor covered it all. Everything happened so fast," I respond as I think back on all of those office visits. She stops interrogating us after accepting the fact that we don't know any more than she does about what happened. Every footstep we take echoes down the desolate hallways. An eerie feeling hangs in the air as we make our way toward the classroom-turned-morgue. As we turn onto the hall where Mr. Panderson's room is, another round of thunder rocks the school. Luckily, the lights stay on this time so no more surprises can happen in the darkness.

"Petunia, can I go ahead and leave? I accidentally forgot to put Teddy back inside the house when I left this morning. He tends to get scared easily in this kind of weather and I can't afford to bring him to the vet if he gets sick," Ms. Zavalla says in a quiet voice, almost at a whisper.

"One of our teachers may be dead and you're worried about a cat getting wet? Are you serious right now, Nellie? Once all of this is over, I think we should start discussing a retirement plan. Your head isn't fully in the game anymore," Principal Blackwater snaps. Ms. Zavalla dips her head in shame as we reach the door to the classroom. I can tell the words really sting her because she's put so many years into this depressing school. The poor old lady isn't ready to let go of the place that's played such a huge part in her life for a long time.

I turn the doorknob to enter the classroom. When I flick on the light, I can instantly tell that something isn't right. The giant window that looks out over the student parking lot is shattered and glass litters the floor. Not a single student stayed behind until we got back with help for Mr. Panderson, which I find incredibly strange. I expected at least a few people to remain behind and wait for us to return.

The desks in the classroom are no longer in rows, but flung up against the walls as if they were tossed by a tornado. The teacher's large wooden desk is splintered into a million pieces. The rolling chair where Mr. Panderson took his last breath is missing two wheels. It looks like a war zone. On the floor where the body was, there is nothing but plain, white tiles.

"Is this some kind of twisted senior prank or did the corpse get up and walk away?" Principal Blackwater turns bright red with anger. "First thing tomorrow, I am getting someone out here to survey all of this damage and both of you will be paying for it. In the meantime, you are both suspended until further notice."

"We're not lying. The body was right there." Trevor points to where the desk was. One large chunk with a leg sticking off it remains. The severed leg is surrounded by hundreds of miniature pieces of wood, covering the floor like maggots on rotting meat.

"Seriously, go back to your office and call some of the students from the class. They'll tell you the same exact story. We weren't the only ones that saw it happen. The room wasn't like this when we left," I say, trying to back up Trevor's pathetic attempt at convincing the principal that we aren't psychotic vandals.

"I plan on contacting the other students and getting to the bottom of this. Maybe the grim reaper came and collected the corpse, then decided to destroy the room. I believe this was a bold faced, fabricated lie. Now, leave the school. I will be getting in touch soon to let both of you know how much the damages come out to be. You two better start saving up those movie theater checks." A diabolical grin washes over the woman's face. She constantly visits our job with her husband and every single time, they leave a huge mess for us to clean up. She snaps at Ms. Zavalla to go and find something to cover the shattered window.

"You are not being fair. We had nothing to do with this. Hell, we were the only ones that even cared enough to come find help. You might want to start your investigation with Caston Wells, since he called the teacher a dick seconds after the man died in front of us. I'm not paying for shit!" My temper rises as Trevor and I back out of the room. It's only been an hour, but this has been the longest and strangest school day ever.

"Now we look absolutely insane. I'm willing to bet money that Caston had something to do with all of this...psychopath," Trevor says as he slams the door shut behind us, leaving the nurse and principal staring in shock at my sudden outburst.

"He's messed up in the head enough to do something like this, but how would he even move the body? He's barely bigger than you," I say to him as we exit the building and descend the stairs to the senior parking lot. The wind has picked up since the last time I was outside and the sky seems to get darker by the second. Plastic bottles and sheets of paper blow across the lot, which is now empty except for my car and his truck. A flash of lightning illuminates the pitch-black clouds.

"I'm sure someone will realize that we're telling the truth when Mr. Panderson doesn't show up for work tomorrow. I'm gonna call Sandra and ask her if she saw anything before she left. I'll let you know what she says. See you at work tonight." He gets inside of his gray pickup truck and drives out of the parking lot.

I'm counting on Sandra to back us up and convince Principal Blackwater that we're telling the truth. I'd really prefer not having to pay to fix a building that I plan on never coming to again since graduation is only a few weeks away. Somehow, this all feels like an elaborate plan of Mr. Panderson's to bring Trevor and I down for good.

CHAPTER 3

Buzz! *Buzz!* The vibration from my phone drags me back to consciousness. The clock on my nightstand reads 3:30 P.M. The storm has given me an opportunity to catch up on some much-needed sleep. Outside of my window, the rain has finally started to come down. The sun is also out, which is a bad omen. I say a silent prayer to myself that no more tragedies happen today. My phone lights up next to the digital clock. Trevor has texted and called me a total of twelve times. I skim over the messages and then call him back.

"Miles, where are you? I've been trying to call you for hours," he says frantically, as if he's about to have a panic attack.

"My bad, I fell asleep. You sound scared. What happened? Did you get in touch with Sandra?" His tone makes my stomach drop. I get up and nervously pace around the room.

"Yes, that's what I've been trying to tell you. She has no memory at all of what happened in the classroom, which means that she can't help us. The last thing she remembers is the lights going out after the thunder. She woke up in her bed at home with no idea of how she got there. I could hear it in her voice that she's telling the truth. She sounded freaked out."

"How is it even possible that she doesn't remember a teacher dying in front of her? Well, now we're dead too. Principal Blackwater is gonna crucify us with those bills."

I've broken into a sweat now as I desperately try to think of a way out of this situation. I save my money to help Mom pay for college, not to fix a damn room for a building that I hate going to.

"It seriously sounded like she had amnesia or something. She also has no idea how the room got trashed. Maybe the wind blew a branch into the glass and we missed it because it was mixed in with the desks." I can imagine him sitting in his room brainstorming ideas that probably sound way better in his head.

"That doesn't explain why it looks like the big desk went through a wood chipper though. I don't know, man. Hopefully we can think of something at work. I gotta go do some homework, I'll see you tonight." I end the call and sit back down on my bed. On top of all of this, I still have assignments to catch up on. It seems like I always have to make a choice between sleeping and homework; there's never a perfect balance between the two. I walk over and flop down in front of the desk in the corner of the room. The screen of my computer lights up when my hand bumps into the mouse.

First up is AP Government. My grade in the class is at a record low for my entire school career. Learning about how this dysfunctional country works hasn't quite piqued my interest. The online textbook is still open from my study session last night. (Okay, I spent more time surfing YouTube for music videos than studying, but that isn't the point.) I need to make at least an eighty-five on the final exam to pull my grade up to barely passing.

Before I can fully delve into the boredom of mass media and special interest groups, a Facebook notification pops up at the top of the screen. KBTY, the local news station, has posted a weather update on the storm that is bearing down on the city. On their page, there is a video of the Doppler radar from the past twelve hours. In the early morning, the radar is completely empty, with not even a speck of green on the map. By noon, the entire state of Texas is covered in red. The most severe line of storms appears to be to the west of Briskwood, slowly but surely making its way in this direction.

The blood colored map is intimidating. At this point, my job should just close for the rest of the day. Deep down, I know it'll never happen. In the two years that I've been at Royal Cinema, we've never closed once. The closest that we've ever gotten to closing our doors on a business day is when a freak ice storm popped up in mid-December last year and bumped back the showtimes by a few hours. Customers completely ignored the fact that the roads were covered in ice and still lined up outside way before we opened. I've come to the conclusion that Hell itself opening up wouldn't be enough to stop the theater from screening the latest and greatest Hollywood films.

My stomach rumbles and I realize that I haven't eaten a thing since that handful of bacon this morning. It's times like these that I really wish fast food restaurants delivered.

Mom is pretty great at keeping the refrigerator stocked with all kinds of foods. Unlike me, she has a strong hatred for fast food and usually tries to make a home-cooked meal at least three times a week. Before I was born, she got food poisoning from eating at a local fast food place and was hospitalized for almost a month. Ever since then, she only eats out in moderation.

Thunder shakes the house as I lazily skim over a paragraph in the online textbook. The emptiness in my stomach distracts me even more than the weather and what happened at school earlier, so I decide to head down to the kitchen and see what Mom has prepared for dinner tonight.

My feet glide over the cold hardwood floors. The light switch for the upper hallway is directly opposite of where I stand right now, so I have to feel my way from my room toward the long spiral staircase. The entire house is bathed in shadows and eerily empty since Mom left for work while I was asleep. The only light comes from the occasional flashes of lightning; otherwise, the rooms are completely dark.

Darkness unsettles me. I always feel like I'm being watched from every angle. The wind howls outside and sounds like a laugh, which only adds fuel to my burning paranoia. A particularly strong gust of wind makes a window creak and the hair on the back of my neck stands up.

There is no way that I'll be able to focus enough to finish studying for AP Government. Oh well, I'm already accepted to Briskwood Community College. It's not like they can retract my acceptance letter if I fail one class. Right?

Inside of the stainless steel refrigerator, Mom has left a pan of my favorite homemade lasagna. I unfold the note that sits on top of the glass dish.

Miles,

Dinner for tonight. I decided to make a quick lasagna since you never took the chicken out of the freezer like I asked you to last night. My sweet, scatterbrained boy. See you when I get off.

Love, Mom.

So that's what she asked me to do last night. I vaguely remember her coming into my room while I was studying, but I didn't bother taking my headphones off to hear what she said.

The cheesy lasagna smells amazing, even though it's freezing cold. I fill up a plate and pop it into the microwave for two minutes. The light from the open refrigerator casts shadows into the living room next to the kitchen. Out of the corner of my eye, I think I see the curtain move slightly, as if someone just brushed past it in a hurry. *Miles, do not walk over there and see if that curtain just moved by itself. You have seen enough horror movies to know that going toward the possible danger never ends well,* I think to myself as I keep my eyes glued to the curtain. Nothing in the living room moves, so I decide that it was just a figment of my imagination. The microwave beeps and I nearly jump out of my skin. It takes every ounce of bravery in my body to turn away from the living room and remove the plate of steaming lasagna.

The winding staircase that leads back to my room looks extra long and uninviting now. With a final glance over my shoulder into the still, dark living room, I walk back up the stairs with my plate of hot dinner.

The only light in my room comes from the Apple logo on the dormant computer screen. I flick on the lamp and slam the door shut. If the curtain moving ax murderer decides to attack me, I've decided that I'd rather not see it coming. The lasagna is delicious and for a brief moment, the swirling winds, magical vanishing teacher, and home invaders leave my thoughts. Good thing it's almost time for me to leave for work. I feel like being surrounded by people, even if those people are customers who seem to get more and more ridiculous as the days go on.

I open up my closet and fumble through the messy, disorganized clothes. After several minutes of searching, I finally find my work uniform. The all black shirt has a large red, black, and green shield plastered onto the back of it since we're currently promoting a new superhero movie that comes out next year. The shirt slides right over my head and I wiggle my way into the black slacks. Droplets of rain pelt the side of my window and remind me to look for an umbrella. I find one in the back of the closet, buried deep below a pile of dirty underwear and T-shirts. It's covered in small holes and looks almost as old as I am, but it'll have to do for now.

I still have forty-five minutes until I have to be at work, but the heavy rain is probably going to cause some serious delays on the freeway. I shrug on the biggest hoodie that I can find over my shirt, grab my keys from the messy desk, and close the door behind me. The darkness of the hallway engulfs my vision once again. This time, my paranoia gets the best of me, so I walk over to the other side of the hallway and turn on the light. My eyes take a few seconds to adjust to the sudden change. The light dissolves the cloud of uneasiness that's been hanging over me ever since the curtain thing happened downstairs.

My beat-up work shoes sit at the top of the staircase and I slip into them before I go back downstairs. I stop on the bottom step and listen before I enter the kitchen. The only sound comes from the rain outside. My car is parked inside the garage and I make sure to set the alarm before I leave, which beeps as it accepts the code that I key in.

I open the door to the garage and find my car in the middle spot of the three parking spaces. The garage is cluttered with boxes of Christmas decorations and old sports equipment that my dad left behind when he deserted his family.

I remember the day everything changed so vividly. When I found out about his unfaithfulness, we were having breakfast at a Denny's. I was sad at first, but it soon turned to anger. The look on Mom's face when she read a text message that popped up on the screen of his phone will probably stick with me for the rest of my life. He accidentally left his phone sitting on the table when he went to use the restroom and she picked it up when it vibrated. On the screen was a text from someone named Emily. To this day, she still won't say exactly what she saw, but it was so bad that she dropped his phone into a glass of water that was on the table. We left the restaurant before he returned from the restroom and he ended up having to call a taxi to bring him home. When he showed up an hour later, Mom already had all of his stuff shoved into trash bags and waiting for him on the front porch. For the next week, he stayed at a trashy motel.

After several failed voicemails trying to convince us of his innocence, he left a strongly- worded letter in our mailbox, blaming Mom for his infidelity. At the end of his explosive rant, he asked for a divorce, said that he would quit his job as a psychologist, and then move to Orlando with the home-wrecker. The spirit slowly drained from my usually positive mom over the first few weeks and she transformed into a person that I didn't recognize. Her constant cheerfulness used to get on my nerves, but I would give anything to be annoyed by it again. Neither of us has spoken to him since that terrible day at the restaurant.

I click the button to unlock my car and hop in. The automatic garage door rises up behind me. I shift into reverse and back out into the thunderstorm. Before I'm even halfway down the driveway, the red 'buckle your seatbelt' light pops up on the dashboard. I click the seatbelt into place, make a right turn onto the street, and head toward the freeway. The sheet of rain comes down so hard that I can barely see anything in front of me.

The low street has already begun to flood. I pass a few smaller cars that are stranded on the side of the road. My muscle car barrels through the rising water, which causes small waves to flow across the street. The droplets of rain hit the windshield as if the heavy clouds above have machine guns attached that propel them down to the ground.

I nearly roll right through a red light that pops up right in front of me. The brakes squeak as my foot slams down on the pedal. I'm worried that the sudden action will cause the car to go sliding into the intersection. Thankfully, the car stops just slightly ahead of the second white line. My old truck probably would've just kept going right into oncoming traffic.

The light turns green after about thirty seconds and I ease off the brakes. To my left, a dark green SUV with a white stripe on the side blasts through the intersection at what must nearly be one hundred miles per hour. The SUV passes just inches in front of me, and the momentum causes my car to rock from side to side. There is no possible way that the driver can see the road going that fast since I can barely see enough to go half the speed limit. I instinctively lay on the horn and scream every curse word that pops into my head. If I had been going at the normal speed like how I usually do when the skies are clear, the SUV would've smashed right into the side of my car and killed me instantly. I lay my head down on the steering wheel to steady my breath. My heartbeat is practically in sync with the raindrops that crash into the windshield less than a second apart. I wipe my sweaty hands on my pants, take a long, deep breath, and finish going through the intersection to get on the freeway.

The traffic isn't nearly as bad I expected it to be and I arrive at work twenty minutes before my shift begins. I remain in the car for ten more minutes, hoping that the rain will slack up a bit. It doesn't. I open up the tattered umbrella that acts more as a filter for the rain than a shield. By the time I reach the covered canopy on the theater, I'm soaked and the heavy rain has torn even larger holes in the umbrella. With a sigh, I toss the useless thing into the trash can in front of the box office.

As I ring out my dripping shirt, I glance out into the parking lot and notice that it isn't nearly as crowded as it usually is. Three rows behind where my car is parked, there is a dark green SUV identical to the one that nearly mowed me down a few minutes ago. The white stripe is clearly visible, even through the downpour. I whip around and fling open the door to the building. Instantly, the strong smell of butter and popcorn hits me right in the face. I knock three times on the door to the box office and a girl with short, black hair peaks her head out.

"Hey Marchelle, did you just sell a ticket to someone driving that green SUV out there?" I point toward the parking lot, even though I'm sure that she can't see anything from right here through the pouring rain.

"I'm not sure what he was driving, but this really weird man just came up and bought a ticket to Mad Max. That's been the only customer I've had for a while. He was acting really twitchy and nervous. That was about ten minutes ago. Why?"

"I think that's the guy who ran a red light and almost killed me on my way here," I say, which makes her eyes widen in surprise. Of course the person who almost just ended my life in a car crash would be going to see a movie that revolves around dangerous driving. Maybe the creep decided to recreate the movie in a wet city in Texas instead of a dry desert in Australia.

"Oh my God. Are you okay? Did he at least try to stop after he ran the light? Should we call the police?" Her voice continuously rises as she asks the questions. She looks genuinely concerned about me and I assure her that I'm okay.

"I'm fine, it just scared me a little. And no, he just kept going like nothing happened. I'm trying to remember if I've ever seen anyone driving an SUV like that around here, but I don't think I have. Anyway, I have to go and clock in now, but thank you," I say as I turn away from her. She mentions that he is wearing all black clothes and a dark green baseball cap just in case I bump into him later and decide to confront him about the reckless driving. After reassuring her several more times that nothing is wrong with me, she closes the door and retreats back into the box office.

I say hello to Ella, who stands at the front taking tickets as the customers come in. It appears to be a slow day, so she's lost in a book and doesn't even look up as I pass. She runs her fingers through her long, brown hair and lets out a deep sigh as she flips a page.

Before I go to the time clock to punch in, I walk over to the restaurant area to grab some paper towels so I can dry myself off. The building is freezing cold and I shiver as I walk down the hallway to the restroom where I can attempt to get some of the water out of my clothes. Fallen popcorn crunches under my wet shoes, which only creates more work for myself. Trevor and Jaden, the other guy who works to-night, don't come in for another hour, so I'm all by myself until then.

I go inside the restroom and awkwardly position my body underneath the hand dryer for a few minutes, which helps a little, but I'm still damp and cold by the time I go to the time clock that sits at the end of a counter down the hall. I peel the hoodie off and toss it into a drawer behind the counter.

Now that my hours are being recorded, it's time to grab a broom and get to work. I walk down the hall, put in the code to the door on one of the storage closets, and grab my favorite broom and dustpan that I use for every shift. I sweep a trail of popcorn that leads back into the lobby like the breadcrumbs from Hansel and Gretel. Ella has the schedules that tell me what time the movies end, so I walk up to her to grab one.

"Can I get a movie schedule?" She's still deeply absorbed into the green-paged book, which I can now see is *Wicked: The Life and Times of the Wicked Witch of the West*.

"Sure, here you go," she says, looking up from the book and handing me the folded paper, just as a customer opens the front door and walks in. Through the glass door, a bolt of lightning comes down in the distance and another round of thunder follows a few seconds later. As the customer gets closer, I realize that I know him.

"Miles. How's it going?" The man walks up to me and shakes my hand. He's my barber, Mr. Fisher.

"I've been pretty good. Ella, this is the man who's responsible for all of this beauty." I turn a finger toward my own face and flash a toothy grin.

"I didn't know your dad left his girlfriend and moved

back from Florida. Hi Mr. Parker, it's nice to meet you." She reaches out and shakes his hand, which is extended to give her his ticket to be torn.

I glare at the back of her head. "This is my barber, Mr. Fisher, not my dad," I say, clearing my throat. She releases his hand and immediately turns red with embarrassment. All three of us fall into an awkward, uncomfortable silence.

"I'm sorry. I feel so stupid. I thought you were talking about genetics, not your haircut," she nervously laughs at herself, "Mr. Fisher, you are going to be in auditorium two today. Enjoy your movie." She gives him back half of his ticket and points down the hallway in the direction of the auditorium where his movie will play.

"See you later, Miles. I'll be expecting a call soon for your next appointment." With a final smile at Ella, he walks up to the restaurant area to buy some food before his movie starts.

The movie schedule tells me that it's almost time to go and clean auditorium nine. A kid's movie plays in there today, so I don't expect there to be much trash since it's a school night. I turn away from Ella and sweep up the lobby before I go down the hall to check on number nine. A single family comes out as I walk up, and the happy credit music fills the hallway through the open double doors. The little girl from the family is excited about the movie, screaming the names of some of the characters, and accidentally bumps into her mom's arm. The remainder of their popcorn spills to the floor.

"I am so sorry about that. This is her first time at the movies," the mom apologizes to me and scoops up her daughter. The cute little girl smiles at me and reveals that she's missing her two front teeth.

"It's no problem at all. Have a good night." I clean up

popcorn and walk into the auditorium to check if there's anyone left. It's empty. I flip on the switch to activate the cleaning lights just as the last animated monkey howls and swings off the screen. I dash up the stairs and find the one row where the family sat. The smashed popcorn takes five seconds to sweep up and I walk back down the stairs.

Weekdays and weekends at this place are polar opposites. On an average Saturday night, it takes between five and seven ushers to clean one auditorium. People really know how to trash a place when they sit in the dark for two hours at a time. I turn off the lights and leave out of the auditorium. Looking down at the schedule, I see that the next movie doesn't end until 6:10. Trevor and Jaden should be here by then, but Trevor is always late, just like at school.

The whole Mr. Panderson situation creeps back into my thoughts. I hope that we can come up with a master plan to prove our innocence to Blackwater. I'm sure that she can contact some of the other students besides Sandra that saw what went down, but she probably wants Trevor and I to scrape together our money to pay for a remodel of the classroom. Sandra is a bit of a party animal so it's possible that she was under the influence of something that wiped her memory, but she seemed totally fine before Trevor and I left to find help. Everything about this is so weird and now that I'm thinking about it again, I can't stop.

In the distance, the lobby looks to be a little more crowded than when I left it, even though the rain shows no signs of ending anytime soon. If I didn't have to be here to work, I would be at home in my warm bed, not out in a thunderstorm to watch a movie.

"Miles, can you please come over here for a second?" I turn around and see a short, skinny man in a suit call after me from down the hallway. He's Mr. Vega, one of the four managers at the theater. He was the first manager that I met when I started and we've become pretty close over the years.

"What's up, Mr. V?" I ask as I walk up to him.

"A customer just came out of Mad Max in number eleven and complained that a man keeps using his cell phone while the movie is going on. Can you go and check it out?" As an usher, it's my job to stop disruptive customers and make sure everyone's movie-going experience is as pleasant as possible.

"Sure. I don't have another movie to clean for another thirty minutes or so. I'll go in there right now."

"Let me know if you run into any problems," he nods at me and walks away in the opposite direction.

Auditorium eleven is a few down from where I stand right now. I've only had to kick people out a couple times since I've been here. First, we're supposed to give the person a warning. If we catch them on the phone again, they get kicked out with no refund. Most people usually comply after the first offense since tickets cost around ten dollars per person on average.

I pull open the door to the auditorium and make my way up the dark incline that leads to the seats. At first glance, I only see about ten people watching the movie and none of them use a phone. I stand there another few minutes, distracted by an intense chase scene that's going on in the movie. Max flies through the desert warding off endless hordes of enemies and the epic guitar music makes the chase seem even more dangerous.

After the scene ends, I reluctantly pry my eyes off of the screen and look back up into the audience. A single light from a phone screen pierces the darkness. Even from down here, the light is so bright that I can clearly see that the per-petrator is a man who wears dark clothes and a baseball cap that has the white Nike logo on it. He perfectly matches the description of the guy that Marchelle described to me earlier and he sits completely alone, which basically confirms that this is the man who almost ended my life.

I go up the stairs and scan each row to make sure no one else is causing a distraction. The man sits directly in the left corner at the top, the part of the auditorium that everyone calls the make out spot. He leans so far over the railing that I think he's going to fall over it, his full attention dedicated to something on the phone screen. His eyes dart from side to side and a layer of sweat covers his forehead.

I reach his seat and lean down to whisper a first and final warning to him, "Excuse me sir, someone has complained that you—"

The man jerks his head up from the phone screen and his eyes widen to the size of dinner plates when he sees me in front of him. He lifts his leg and a black boot connects with my stomach, which sends me flipping backwards over the railing. The kick knocks the air from my lungs before I have a chance to scream. I reach my arms to out to grab onto something, but it's too late. The floor below rapidly approaches and I close my eyes before impact.

CHAPTER 4

"M iles! Miles!" I gasp and sit up too fast, which sends a piercing wave of pain shooting through my head. Someone lays me back down, tells me to stay still, and then places an ice pack on my forehead. My vision is blurred and I can't see anything around me. After a few seconds, my eyes clear up some-what and I realize that I'm on the old green couch in the break room upstairs. Mr. Vega and Trevor stand above me. I almost don't see Jaden leaning up against the wall behind them. His pale skin almost blends in with the blank canvas of the break room walls. They all look scared at first, and then relieved when I open my mouth to talk.

"Wh-what happened?" I manage to stutter out.

"You took a pretty nasty fall from the top of number eleven. You've been out cold for almost two hours. A paramedic came by a little while ago to check your vitals, but he decided that it wasn't severe enough to bring you to the hospital. You regained consciousness for a few minutes when you were getting checked out, but fell asleep shortly after that. We moved you up here so you could rest up for a bit," Mr. Vega explains and suddenly everything rushes back to me. The look of sheer terror on the man's face when I tried to tell him to put the phone away, then his foot smashing into my stomach, and falling over the railing toward the floor at what felt like the speed of light.

"A man did this. I think he's really out to get me," I whis-per to myself.

"What was that?" I snap my head up too fast, which sends another wave of pain through my skull. I'm met with concerned looks from Trevor and Mr. Vega when I grimace.

"A man in an SUV flew through a red light and almost hit me on my way here. The same man was the one who kicked me over the railing when I went to tell him to put his phone away. Ask Marchelle about it, she sold him a ticket and said that he was acting really weird," I say. If I ever see that man again, I'll kick his ass. I don't care that I might end up in jail or with a huge fine on top of the damage to the classroom that I already might have to pay.

"She got off about an hour ago, but I'll make sure to call her later. Do you want to go home for the rest of the night? We're not busy at all. Trevor and Jaden should be able to handle the auditoriums by themselves and I'll be here to help out as well," Mr. Vega says, resting a supportive hand on my shoulder.

"Nah, it's fine. I actually feel pretty normal, but I would love some water."

I'm glad number eleven isn't that big. If this would've happened in number one or nine, the larger auditoriums, I would be in much worse shape right now. I don't want to go home and miss out on any money, especially since I'll probably end up having to pay Blackwater if she goes through with her threat.

"Trevor, run downstairs and grab your friend some water." Mr. Vega turns away from me to my best friend. Trevor leaves the break room and a few seconds later, the elevator rumbles up the shaft to get him so he can ride down to the ground floor.

"You really had me scared, man," Jaden says, speaking for the first time since we've been in the room. I don't know him all that well because he's only been working here for about a month and we've only had a handful of shifts together.

"Thanks a lot for helping move me up here. It means a lot." I take the ice pack off of my head and sit it on the floor.

"No problem," he glances down at his movie schedule, "I have to run downstairs and check on a few movies that are about to end. See you in a few." Mr. Vega thanks him for helping move me up here and he leaves the room.

"Are you positive that you want to stay? I promise that I won't be upset if you need to leave and rest some more." Mr. Vega is pushing for me to go home, but I reassure him that I'm okay when I stand and take a few steps. My feet are asleep and it takes a few seconds for the tingling to go away, but other than that I feel completely fine. There's only three more hours until I get off at 11:00. I should be able to finish the rest of my shift with no problems.

"Do you have any idea where that man disappeared to after he went all Jackie Chan on me?" My fists have a couple of not so nice words to say to the man's face. I crack my knuckles.

"I didn't even know that there was someone who caused you to fall over. After the movie ended, a customer came out and said that one of the employees was unconscious on the floor. I guess no one saw you fall because of how dark and loud it was in the auditorium. I turned on the cleaning lights and walked up to where it looked like you fell from. I found a wet spot on the floor right above you and just assumed that you slipped. I would say that we should call the police, but I'm sure they won't see this as a real emergency. Since you're not seriously hurt, it's not worth it," he says. Strange. I don't remember seeing any wet spots, but everything happened so fast that I could've easily missed it. Maybe the creep knocked over his drink when he fled the scene of the crime.

We leave the break room and press the arrow on the elevator to go back down. The elevator travels up the shaft and opens up, where we find Trevor inside with a cold bottle of water in his hands. I grab it from him and chug the whole thing before the doors even close to bring us back down.

"There's the Miles I know and love. For a second there, I thought you pulled a Panderson," Trevor says, making light of the situation far too soon. Still, I have to stop a smile from forming on my face and answer to Mr. Vega's confused look.

"It's a very long and weird story. I don't even know how to explain it to you," I say to answer the manager's puzzled expression. We reach the bottom floor and the elevator slides open. There is a line outside at the box office that almost extends past the covered canopy into the thunderstorm. The rain still hasn't let up at all in the two hours that I've been unconscious.

"Looks like you'll have to tell me about it later." Mr. Vega walks away from us, toward the box office to help whoever's in there cut down the long line. Hopefully he forgets to ask about Mr. Panderson. The last thing I need is another adult, especially a manager at my job, to think that I'm crazy.

I pull the crumpled movie schedule out of my pocket to check where we're headed to next. Jaden should be cleaning number seven right now. I pick up a broom and dustpan that's against the wall next to the elevator. Trevor and I make our way through the packed lobby, sweep up piles of spilled popcorn, and then travel to the other side of the building. Jaden is rolling the gray trash can out of the auditorium as we walk up.

"This one is all good. Next up is number four. After we do that one, it'll be time for me to go on break," he says as he walks past us, down the hall to put the trash can inside of the next auditorium that we'll clean on this side since we never cross the lobby with them.

A couple years before I applied to work here, one of the employees brought a can through the lobby and instead of paying attention to what was in front of him, he was texting. An old lady pushing a walker came into the lobby from the auditorium that she was in to refill her popcorn tub. The employee accidentally pushed the can right into the old lady's walker and made her tumble to the ground. The lady ended up with a broken hip, not from the fall itself, but from when the employee tripped over the fallen walker and landed on top of her. The employee ended up with a cracked phone screen and no job. Ever since then, we haven't been allowed to bring the cans across the lobby.

Before we go back over to the side that we just came from with Mr. Vega, I take a slight detour to the front entrance to take a peek outside to see if the green SUV is still in the parking lot. The lot has way more cars in it than the last time I saw it, so I can't tell if the man is still parked three rows behind me. Before I can walk out into the storm to get a better look, the sky lets out a round of thunder so strong that it shakes the huge theater. The lights flicker off for a split second, but hopefully not long enough to screw up the movie projectors upstairs. I turn around and go back to Trevor, who stands at the front talking to Ella. I'm finally dry from earlier and I don't want to get wet again to look for the man who assaulted me.

"Come on, T. Let's go check on number four and not make Jaden do all of the work tonight." We walk away from

Ella and go through the lobby to the side of the building that holds auditoriums one through eight. Jaden rolls the gray trash can into number four, and then turns the corner going toward the exit door at the back of the auditorium.

I turn to Trevor to initiate our brainstorming about what happened at school earlier. "So about this Mr. Panderson thing...have you thought of any way to convince Blackwater that we haven't lost our minds?" His ever-present smile fades and I know the answer before he even opens his mouth.

"Nope. But I have started making a list of things that I'm gonna give away to people while I'm in prison," he says with a shallow smirk, but his eyes reveal that he is just as scared as I am.

"I'd say that our best bet is to just wait it out and pray that someone from the class tells her what really went down. It just sucks that this could've easily been solved if the stupid old classroom had cameras."

"Technology," he nods in agreement. We go inside number four only to find that the credits are still rolling. Jaden hangs out of the exit door, waiting for the remaining customers to come out so we can clean before the next showing starts. When we walk in, he calls us over to him.

"Guys, come here! Something's wrong," Jaden shouts. We go over to where he is and peak out the door. On the ground outside, there are about a dozen motionless black birds. They all lie on their sides, with lifeless, beady black eyes that stare up into the dark sky above. The two that are closest to me have cracked beaks, which means that they most likely fell from high up in the air. All of them are soaked from the rain and their feathers are slicked down like they're covered in hair gel.

"What the hell? It's really time for this day to be over, it keeps getting weirder and weirder," I say as chills pop up on my arms because of the grisly sight. I reach out and tap one of the stiff bodies with the end of my broom.

"What did you do, Jaden? At least we don't have to buy food on our breaks now. Pop one of these in the microwave and we'll be good to go." No one laughs at Trevor's joke this time.

Lightning fills the gloomy sky, which perfectly fits the mood for the scene outside. The roads must be flooded by now and I don't want to drive home, even in my powerful muscle car.

I peel my eyes away from the dead birds when I realize that the auditorium has fallen silent and that the credits have ended. "The credits are over. We can clean up the birds after we finish in here," I say as Trevor snaps pictures of the birds on his phone.

"After we get done, I'm gonna go find Mr. Vega to show him these pictures and ask where we should put these. I would think that they go inside of the compactor, but I've never actually had to dispose of dead birds before," Trevor says, locking his phone and slipping it back into his pocket.

Trevor and I go ahead of Jaden to the seating area as he turns on the lights so we can see what we need to clean. Trevor picks up a golden pocket watch from a cup holder on the top row of seats and stops on the staircase to examine it. "It has a skull on it." He turns it over. "Someone's initials are engraved onto the back of it. I'm gonna go turn this in to the box office, I bet the person will come back for it. Hopefully Mr. Vega is still in there so I can show him these pictures." He runs down the stairs and leaves the auditorium.

Jaden looks down at his watch. "Well, time for my break. Have fun with the dead animal clean up." He pats me on the back twice and walks out behind Trevor. I turn off the lights and walk back over to the exit door to wait for Trevor.

I crack the door open to watch the rain hit the concrete. As I stare at the back of the building, I think I see a blur disappear around the corner in the time that it takes me to blink once. The moving curtain from the living room pops into my head. Of course my eyes would play tricks on me again right before Trevor and I will probably have to go alone to the compactor. I lift my shirt up to wipe my eyes and stick my head out into the cool rain to clear my thoughts a bit.

Trevor bursts back into the auditorium a few minutes later and scares me right out of my trance. He carries a roll of black trash bags and box of disposable gloves. The strong smell of latex fills my nose when he opens up the box and pulls out two pairs of them for us. I decide not to tell him about the figure that I think I saw disappear to the back of the building. It's better not to think about things like that when we have to go back there and get the job done no matter what.

"Mr. V said that we should bag up the birds and toss them in the compactor. We can use a couple of these bags as rain ponchos so we don't get as soaked." He pulls off two of the bags from the roll. We open up the bags and pop holes in them so we can stick our heads and arms through. With the ponchos in place, we slide our hands into the gloves.

The skintight gloves, combined with the cheap trash bag scrubs, make us look like evil doctors straight out of a horror movie. Now that we're fully geared up and ready to go, we step out into the howling storm. I look around for something to stick in the door so we can get back in.

Trevor shouts over the wind when he notices what I'm

doing, "You don't have to worry about that. Mr. V gave me his keys to the building because he thinks the wind is gonna blow away anything you stick in the door to keep it open." He pulls a ring of shiny keys out of his pocket as I let go of the door and let the wind slam it shut.

"Dude, you don't have to shout that loud. We're not inside of a tornado," I say. He glares at me and opens up another bag for us to put the birds in.

I reach down and grab two of the cold animals that lie at my feet. The stiff and rubbery creatures land at the bottom of the bag that Trevor holds open when I toss them in. He leans down and plucks two of them from the ground by their wings, which causes bones to snap loudly. He catches me staring at him with my eyes narrowed.

"What? They're dead, it's not like they can feel it. Do you think the compactor is gonna stroke their feathers and sing them a lullaby?" He says with a chuckle.

"No, but I won't be able to see the compactor smash their bones. Smart ass." We pick up the remaining few birds in silence.

After I place the last one into the bag, Trevor ties it off and we walk toward the back of the building where the compactor is. The wind behind the building is much stronger and a gust causes the half-empty bag to billow behind Trevor like a cape. Back here, a few of the lights on the building are out and others are extremely dim. The temperature feels like it's dropped at least twenty degrees since the last time I came outside, which is really weird considering that summer starts in a few weeks. Chills rise up all over my body underneath the trash bag poncho.

I appreciate what Jaden did for me after my incident earlier, but it was so wrong of him to go on break and leave the dirty work for Trevor and I to do. A twinge of jealousy rises inside of me when I picture him relaxed on the couch in the warm break room while I stand outside wet and cold.

"Is it just me or is it way too cold out here for it to be mid-May?" Trevor pulls the words right out of my thoughts. Mom didn't mention anything about a cold front this morning. She would've definitely told me to take a jacket with me if she knew about it. Even though Briskwood always has unpredictable weather, usually in the form of a random thunderstorm that pops up at the most inconvenient times, but a complete seasonal change in the span of a few hours has never happened before.

I nod my head in agreement, "Yeah, it really is. I don't know what's going on today, man. Weird stuff back to back to back."

We're about halfway to the huge gray compactor when a bolt of lightning comes down about twenty feet in front of us. Trevor yelps as every light on the building around us explodes. My heart is about to beat out of my chest. A few lights remain intact, but they're way ahead of us and it creates the illusion of us being trapped in a long tunnel with a glimmer of hope at the very end. In the darkness, my mind automatically goes back to the blur I'm pretty sure I saw come back here a few minutes ago. I try to lock the thought in a door at the back of my head, but the darkness plows through it like a bulldozer.

I lift the poncho and fumble around in my pocket for my phone. I grab it and turn on the flashlight. "That was really close. Let's just make a run for it so we can get back inside," I shout to Trevor as he shields his eyes from the bright flashlight. We run the rest of the way to compactor in ten seconds, while the wind pushes back on us for every exhausting stride. The lights on this side of building are still lit, so I turn off the light on my phone and slip it back into my pocket.

When I reach out to grab the handle to open up the compactor, I realize that my hands are so cold that I can barely feel them. Trevor spins around twice and launches the bag of dead birds into the empty compactor, where they land at the bottom with a thud.

With the birds inside of their sticky and disgusting resting place, I slam the door shut. Trevor takes a few steps toward the compactor.

"Should we say a few words?" He closes his eyes and folds his hands as if he's about to break out into a prayer. I walk over and slap him at the back of the head.

"Come on, let's go back inside before another bolt of lightning comes down and puts us in there with them." I wonder if he can tell that I'm in no mood to put up with his jokes tonight.

I walk away from him to go back toward the patch of darkness where the lightning blew the lights out. A high-pitched scream from some kind of animal fills the night. It's loud enough to be heard over the wind and sounds like it came from the woods behind the theater. Trevor stands right where I left him, eyes glued to something that I can't see from where I stand.

"Miles, come over here." His voice is barely above a whisper and I almost can't hear him over the strong wind. I walk back to him and squint my eyes toward the spot where he looks. About halfway up a tree a few rows deep into the woods, a pair of glowing yellow eyes stare back at us. From here, it's too dark inside the dense collection of trees for me to make out what the eyes belong to.

"Did you see what kind of animal that is?" I'm sure that he probably didn't. There's a decent sized parking lot behind the theater that separates us from the woods. Since Briskwood is a rural city, we have a lot of wild animals that roam around here.

"Yeah. It was a werewolf," he says with a straight face and then his top lip quivers. About thirty seconds later, he bursts out laughing so hard that he doubles over. "The look on your face was priceless."

I turn my head back to the woods just as the eyes blink and then retreat deeper into the trees. Hopefully, it was just a curious raccoon that was waiting for us to drop a few bags of popcorn for its dinner. I've seen a family of them back here before, late at night. That also probably explains the blur I saw while I waited for Trevor. Maybe the raccoon spotted me and then ran back to its home in the woods.

"Wait up!" Trevor's voice echoes behind me, but I'm already far ahead of him and don't want to hear more of his jokes. The wind propels me forward since I don't walk against it anymore. I reach the door to go back inside in way less time than it took to get to the compactor.

I'm so used to having something hold the door open that I forget Trevor has the keys to get back in. I lean up against the cold wall and wait for him to join me. I pull out my phone to check the radar, but keep it under the poncho so the rain doesn't destroy it. It looks like the weather system is finally on its way out of the area. The waves of rain that remain are yellow on the radar, with only a few specks of red mixed in.

I close out of the radar and tap the Twitter app. I refresh my timeline and it fills with the usual tweets that I see every time I come on here: students complaining about school, a reality TV star gave birth yet again, people posting their favorite generic song lyrics. I almost scroll past a breaking news post from CNN because it's right below someone that is complaining about a relationship they've been in for less than a week. I click the link to the article in their tweet and it brings me to the CNN website.

According to them, the severe weather isn't just isolated to Briskwood. Storms batter most of Texas, Los Angeles, New York City, Chicago, and a ton of other major cities as well. Power outages are being reported from all over the country and millions of people are currently without electricity. Toward the bottom of the article, it says that meteorologists are confused by the random appearance of severe weather all over the country at the same time. The forecasts for most of the cities called for clear skies for the next few days. They describe the severe weather as dangerous and unpredictable, and warn people not to go outside unless it's absolutely necessary. Right on cue, another round of deafening thunder booms through the sky.

Trevor walks up just as I finish reading the news article. All of the color is drained from his face. "What's wrong with you now?" I decide to give him one more chance to be serious before I punch him in the stomach.

"I saw what those floating yellow eyes belong to. It was this...thing. It popped out literally as soon as you jogged away. I couldn't even call after you because when I saw it, I forgot how to talk," he trembles. Unless he somehow learned how to act in the past five minutes, I think what he says is true. He doesn't burst out laughing after thirty seconds this time. He uses his shaky hands to pull Mr. Vega's keys out of his pocket to get us back inside of the building, but he can't seem to focus enough to get the key into the slot on the door. I take the ring of keys from him and open it myself. We walk back inside and the door slams shut behind us, sealing us in from whatever dangers are outside.

"What exactly did it look like?" The trailers before the movie inside number four have already started to play again. We've been outside for a little longer than I thought.

"Well, it was pretty far away, so I'm not one hundred per-cent sure. From where I stood, it looked like a guy that had these black spikes sticking out all over his body. It didn't look like he was wearing any clothes either. He moved so fast that I wasn't able to see much, but those eyes...man, those eyes." I grab the rolling trash can, which almost runs over with garbage. We walk out of auditorium four and back into the hallway, where I leave the can by the door. Since Jaden thought it would be cool to leave us and go on break, I decide that he gets to take out the trash on his own. I pick up my broom from where it leans on the wall and sweep crushed popcorn from the floor.

Something tells me that Trevor isn't making this up, but I still have to make sure he isn't being paranoid. "Are you sure that it wasn't just a really big raccoon? Maybe the spikes were just a trick of the light."

"I didn't know that raccoons walked on their back legs and grew to be six feet tall. Must be a newly discovered breed," he snaps back at me. I feel a headache coming on from all of the nonsense that I've had to endure today: a dead, disappearing teacher, a customer that tried to kill me, and a human porcupine. This day needs to be over already.

We've almost made it back to the lobby when Jaden comes down the elevator from the break room. He finishes the last bite of his burger before he comes toward us.

"Should we tell him about what you saw?" I motion toward Jaden and whisper in Trevor's ear.

"No, I'm not even positive that it wasn't just some creep playing around in a costume. I don't want anyone to think that I've lost my mind," he says.

"What's up guys? Where are we headed to next?" Jaden walks up to us. I completely forgot about the auditoriums that we might have missed while we were outside on dead bird disposal duty. I pull the damp, crumpled movie schedule from my back pocket and discover that luckily, we had a huge break in between number four and number thirteen, the next one that ends.

"We just got back inside from taking out the birds. No movies have ended since you've been on break. We're gonna head to number thirteen since it's about to end," I say to him as he walks in the direction that we just came from, to go to the restroom before he clocks back in.

"Oh yeah. Tell me about how that went once I meet back up with y'all. The burger was so amazing that I forgot about the dead birds," he calls back over his shoulder.

"I bet you did. Loser," Trevor mutters under his breath, where only I can hear what he says.

"Look, let's focus and try to put all of this weirdness behind us. Time to go clean number thirteen." The strongest thunder of the night suddenly hits and it sounds like the world will split open. I really hope the radar wasn't wrong, but I'm starting to have my doubts.

We cross the lobby and I pull out my phone to check the time. It's already 9:00. In two more hours, it'll be time for me to go home. Down the hall, number thirteen has just let out and I can already tell that the auditorium will be trashed from the herd of people that stand outside of it.

A large group of customers huddle up right outside of the door. As we get closer, it becomes clear that the group is gathered around a tall dark haired man who shows them something on his phone. Someone in the crowd gasps.

"What is that thing? Where is it taking her? Oh my God, I can't watch this," a person in the crowd says. A short, pudgy lady with curly blonde hair stands at the edge of the crowd. I tap her on the shoulder.

"Excuse me, ma'am. What's going on?" She turns around and stares at me with puffy, red eyes that leak black mascara all down her cheeks. Behind her, the rest of the crowd stares at the phone screen with looks of shock and disbelief on their faces.

"There's an attack happening right now in Los Angeles. This man got a notification about it as we walked out of the movie. People have transformed into these animals or something that have taken over the city. According to the news, it started about thirty minutes ago when the rain changed to a dark red color and infected anything it touched. Right now, it's stopped raining, but the damage is already done. They're vicious and destroying everything in sight." The woman is barely able to get out the last few words before she returns to her weeping. Trevor makes his way through the crowd to get a better look at the man's phone.

"Come over here, Miles," he says when he looks down at the screen. His face is expressionless as I weave through the bodies and go to him. When I reach him, he grabs my arm with his sweat-drenched hand and drags me into the auditorium we're supposed to clean right now.

"Hey! What are you doi—"

"The creature in the news story on the man's phone looks just like the one I saw when we went to the compactor. I would recognize those scary yellow eyes anywhere," he says with a gulp. As if to confirm his testimony, a clap of thunder rolls in the distance. The auditorium is completely empty, but he whispers in my ear so the people that stand right outside of the door don't hear us.

"Are you serious? I wonder why the one we saw didn't attack us. This is crazy. Do you think it's an alien invasion?" I say it jokingly, but the way today is going, I wouldn't be too surprised if it turned out to be true.

I go back to the CNN website on my phone. The breaking news about the attack is all over the homepage. This story is brand new. It wasn't mentioned anywhere on the website when I read about the severe weather a few minutes ago. I press play on the video that's in the article and immediately, a warning for graphic content pops up. The video plays after the warning and shows surveillance footage from one of the buildings in downtown Los Angeles. The grainy camera films the traffic filled street. All of a sudden, the creature flies into the frame and lands on top of one of the vehicles in the line of cars. At first, it moves so fast that it's a blur and I can't make out any of its features.

The roof of the car is dented when the pointy creature springs from the top of it and lands gracefully on the ground. I can tell that the hulking monster was once a man, with spikes that erupt out of his large biceps. He saunters up to the taxi as if he has all the time in the world to get to where he needs to go. The skin of the beast is gray in color underneath all of those long, pointy spikes that jut out from all over his body. Spikes even come out of the back of the thing's head and curve down his back to create an illusion of extremely long hair. A tie is around his neck and pieces of a tattered business suit hang off of the spikes, which reminds me of how trees look when they get toilet papered on Halloween.

People try desperately to snap pictures and record videos of the scene on their phones, but still stay far enough away from the creature to not be in immediate danger. The creature raises his nose to the sky and sniffs the air like a predatory animal as he circles the taxi. He leans his head back and lets out a bloodcurdling sound that strongly resembles a mixture of lion's roar and a wolf's howl. A chill races up my spine. Razor sharp teeth line the inside of the creature's mouth. They look like they can bite through metal as if it is melted butter.

He steps up to the taxi, reaches out with a grotesque hand, and then embeds four of the spikes into the back passenger door. With a single tug, the door unhinges from the car and ricochets off of a bus before it smashes through the glass window of a McDonald's. The people that snap pictures of the monster immediately stop and then run down the packed street in a disorganized mob. A lady even hurtles over one of the parked cars, obviously trying to put as much distance between herself and the creature as possible.

The creature gets distracted by the fleeing crowd for a split second, but immediately turns his wild eyes back to the taxi. He reaches into the back seat and plucks a screaming, leggy woman out with ease. In the creature's arms, the terrified lady looks tiny and helpless. She yells at the top of her lungs and begs the creature to let her go. Her arms and legs flail as she tries to escape from his tight grasp. Then, he rotates his head and looks directly into the surveillance camera. His thin, leathery lips curl into an evil half smile. The soulless yellow eyes stare right at me, and then the camera feed fades into static.

Trevor and I are speechless as we absorb what we just saw. I decide that it's time to break the silence after a few seconds. "Exactly what did I just watch?" My voice comes out a lot shakier than I expect it to.

"It looks like the beginning of the end to me," I say. The video replays over and over in my head. The face of the doomed woman from the taxi is permanently stamped into my thoughts.

"I guess now would be a great time to tell Mr. Vega about what you saw out back. This dirty auditorium is gonna have to wait. I think he'll understand if anyone complains about it, but I doubt anyone will even come to the next showing. Not with this going on," I say as we turn around and walk right back out into the hallway. Only a few people from the crowd still remain by the door of the auditorium. The tall man with the phone, the bearer of bad news, is gone. The crying lady stands by a water fountain that's next to the restroom as she wipes stray tears from her eyes with a tissue. A dark thought pops into my head out of nowhere. If there is some kind of apocalypse that's about to take place, she won't last long unless she toughens up and fast. I've waited for something like this to happen for almost my entire life and I think I'm prepared enough to last at least a year or two if the world ends. We leave them behind and continue up the hallway into the lobby.

Ella still stands up front tearing tickets hours later. Her book is flipped over to mark her place while she assists customers that, surprisingly, are still coming in. "Ella, we have to tell Mr. Vega something right now. Have you seen him?" I ask.

"He walked down the hallway a few minutes. He might've gone upstairs. I'm not sure," she says and points in the direction of the elevator.

"Awesome. You're the best." Trevor pats her on the back and we walk away from her to the hallway to look for the manager. The number two above the elevator is lit up, which means that he's most likely upstairs in the office. I turn to Trevor.

"So, what do you wanna do? Wait until he comes down or run up the stairs to tell him?" The elevator is locked from the bottom so nosy customers don't wander around in the projection booth upstairs.

Trevor and I created this rumor about a man that went up there and got electrocuted by one of the projectors. When we train new employees, we always make sure to mention how his ghost haunts the booth and they usually fall for it every single time. We even made up some convincing fake stories and victims to back up the urban legend. Xiomara, a box office cashier who snuck up there with her boyfriend one night after she got off and was never heard from again. Andrew Princeton, a roof inspector who mysteriously slipped from the top of the building while he was doing some maintenance.

"I think we should just wait down here. Suddenly, I can't remember the passcode to get into the office," I've been friends with Trevor for long enough to know when he isn't passionate about doing something. He's a good worker most of the time, but add in extra work like climbing a flight of stairs for a reason that may or may not be an emergency? That's a different story. Plus, I'm sure that he knows I have the code to the office. I decide not to argue because my head now throbs painfully and I don't want to climb a flight of stairs any more than he does. Mr. Vega should be down soon anyway.

"Fine. I guess we can just chill right here and let those things take over the world. No big deal," I say, glaring at him.

"Don't be so pessimistic. Whatever this is will blow over by tomorrow. You know how these things go," he says, but I don't think it will. Blood red rain doesn't just fall from the sky and turn people into mutants. In a large city like Los Angeles, cops are everywhere. The thing would be surrounded instantly if the officers knew how to handle something like this. The fact that I saw no police officers in that CNN video tells me that they're just as confused and scared about the situation as we are. I guess they've seen enough end of the world movies to know that surrounding the monster with only pistols never ends well. They're most likely waiting for the big guns to figure out what the hell is going on before springing into action.

I glance down the hall and notice that the full trash can I left by auditorium four isn't there anymore. I stop Trevor, who still rambles and tries to convince me (and probably himself) that tomorrow everything will be back to normal.

"Do you think Jaden already went to take out that can? He shouldn't be back there alone. We should go and check on him," I say, nodding my head in the direction of where I left the can.

"He didn't help us with the dead birds. Why should we help him?" Trevor grumbles. I can't believe he's still mad over something so petty when this might be a life or death situation.

"Maybe because there might be something out there that wants to rip him to pieces. Come on," I say. We walk down the hall headed to number four just as Jaden walks back inside. We're still about ten feet away so I call out to him.

"Hey man, we were just about to—" My voice catches in my throat. From farther away, he looks totally normal, but as we get closer, I get the sinking feeling that something isn't right. Popcorn tubs and cups still peak out of the top of the full trash can, which means that he never made it around back to the compactor. A huge puddle of liquid around his feet darkens the patterned carpet where he stands. At first, I think he's soaking wet because of the rain. When I get even closer, it becomes clear that red liquid covers every inch of his skin that isn't clothed.

The red liquid drips from his usually neat black hair, which is now messily scattered all over his head. Two strings of hair stick down diagonally on his forehead, which makes it look like he has horns. He doesn't say a word, in fact it seems like he doesn't even realize that we stand right in front of him.

"Dude, what the—" Trevor starts, but never gets to finish. Jaden's eyes roll into the back of his head and he collapses to the ground.

CHAPTER 5

Instinct takes over and I rush to the spot where Jaden lies unconscious of the floor. I reach down to check his pulse, but a pair of hands grab me from behind and pull me backwards. Trevor drags me away, his eyes wide with fear. "Do you not remember what that lady told us about how the rain changed to red before those creatures appeared in the city? That might not be his blood. Hell, it might not even be blood at all. We can't touch him."

"We need gloves," I agree. I almost forgot what the lady said about the red rain. A chill runs up my spine when I realize that I almost got some of that stuff on my skin.

"I'll go get some. You stay here and make sure nobody messes with him." Trevor jogs off down the hall to find where he left the box of gloves after we moved the birds earlier. I look back to Jaden's motionless body on the floor. When I stare a little harder, I can see his chest rise and fall underneath the wet, black shirt that sticks to him like a new layer of skin.

I had been holding my breath and my muscles were tensed up, but now that I know he's still breathing, I relax just a little. He looks terrible and I need to do something besides stand here and watch over him, but I can't be much help at all without the gloves. It's way too risky.

I sit down against the wall and sigh. I wonder if Mr. Vega is still upstairs. He needs to come down so I can tell him about everything that's happened. As much as I hate to think about it, Jaden could transform into one of those things any minute now and we need to prepare for it. The last thing that we need to happen today is a monster terrorizing families who are out to enjoy a movie. I'm sure Mr. Vega will agree that quarantine will be the best option until we can figure out another way to handle this situation.

Another earthshaking round of thunder hits and the lights don't stay on this time. Either the radar lied to me or more lines of thunderstorms have formed out of nowhere. My heartbeat picks up when I realize that I sit in the dark right next to someone that I'm supposed to watch over, but also someone that may end my life in a few minutes. I take a deep breath and try to calm myself down. "He'll be perfectly fine. Don't think like that," I say out loud to myself. There is no light whatsoever. We may as well be inside of a cave.

I use the flashlight on my dying phone to look around. The red liquid all over Jaden's skin still hasn't dried at all. He's just as soaked as he was when he came inside a few minutes ago. Actually, he looks even wetter, as if he is still outside in the downpour. The liquid looks exactly like blood, thick and dark. If I didn't know any better, I would assume that he was just pulled from the wreckage of a terrible car accident. He's only missing the cuts and broken bones.

I scoot across the floor and get as close as I possibly can without actually touching him. I lean down and stare at one of the individual droplets on his face. This close up, the liquid is not purely red in color, but has tiny black dots that swirl around inside of each droplet. I feel chills rise up on my arms again and I nearly gag. A droplet of the liquid trickles down his face and rolls off the top of his lip into his slightly open mouth. When the droplet touches his tongue, he gasps.

His limbs spasm and I have to awkwardly jump back with my butt to avoid getting showered by the liquid that flies off of him. His entire body shakes, as if electricity courses through his veins. My phone slips from my hand and bounces across the floor when I spring to my feet. Darkness takes over once again and for a moment, the only thing I can see is the small light coming from my phone that has landed a few feet away from where Jaden seizes on the floor. When he gurgles loudly, I picture white foam running out of his mouth, mixing in with the red liquid and transforming his pale face into a pink art canvas.

I retrieve my phone from the floor and shine the light over him. He's still unconscious even though his head violently thrashes into the ground. No foam comes out of his mouth, which is now completely shut closed.

As quickly as the seizure starts, it ends. The spasms stop, he goes limp, and his chest rises and falls at the normal pace once again. I breathe out a sigh of relief, but still shine the light over him just in case. Trevor jogs up a minute later, the light from his own phone bounces up and down in the dark corridor until he stops in front of me.

"Got the gloves. Mr. Vega was in the lobby and I filled him in on everything. He's on the phone with the power company right now to see how long the lights will be out. He's about to call the paramedics for Jaden and come down here once he gets off the phone. He seems kinda pissed that we didn't go upstairs to get him sooner. Did Jaden wake up at all yet?" He tosses me the box of gloves after he rips two free for himself.

"He just had a seizure. Some of that stuff got into his mouth and he freaked out. It only lasted like thirty seconds, but it felt way longer," I say. Trevor's eyes widen under the bright light from his phone and he reminds me of a boy scout who is about to tell a scary story by a campfire.

"This happened in the five minutes that I walked away? Aw man, I always miss the action," he says disappointedly.

"It was scary. I couldn't even reach down and try to help him since I couldn't touch his skin or wet clothes. Oh and the liquid isn't completely red. It has weird black circles inside of the droplets," I say, filling him in on my observation. Jaden groans below us and for a second, I think he's about to wake up.

His eyes still do not open, but the liquid on his skin bubbles like a pot of boiling water on a stove. He screams out in pain and thin wisps of steam rise from face. The liquid seeps down into his skin, absorbs into him as if he is a human sponge. He seizes again, even harder than the last time. I reach down now that I have gloves on and try to stop his head from smacking into the ground. Even through the gloves, his skin is hot to the touch.

Trevor stands in shock, watching over us. "Go get Mr. Vega right now. Drag him here by the few strands of his hair that are left if you have to!" I scream at him. Jaden coughs so hard that I wouldn't be surprised if a lung popped out of his mouth and hit me in the face. When the rest of the red liquid seeps down into his open pores, my stomach seems to rumble as loudly as the thunder outside. I have to turn away from him before I throw up.

After the last of the liquid is gone, he stops shaking and lies still on the filthy, stained carpet. His skin goes back to its regular porcelain white color. A sigh escapes from his mouth and then his chest stops rising and falling. I peel the glove off of my right hand and stick it underneath his nose. The tickle of his exhaled breath isn't there. I slide my hand back into the glove and push on his chest, as I hope and pray that I can bring him back without touching my lips to his.

"Help! He isn't breathing!" I shout down the hallway in between chest compressions. I have no idea if this is helping him or hurting him even more since I'm not certified in CPR, but I have to try something. I regret not listening to Mom's requests for me to take a certification class. Now, I wish she would've forced me to do it. I yell down the hallway until Trevor returns with an out of breath Mr. Vega.

"Do either of you know how to do CPR? He's not breathing," I shout as they approach me.

Mr. Vega drops down on his knees and pushes me aside. "We're on our own. The paramedics have suspended all services until this freak rain clears up. Trevor tells me that the stuff just drained into his skin? How peculiar." He examines Jaden's face before he picks up where I left off with the CPR. My pathetic attempt probably caused more harm than good. After he does several chest compressions, he presses his lips against Jaden's mouth and blows air into his lungs. I think to myself that this is a brave move, to put his lips on a person who just absorbed God knows what into his body.

I'm so focused on Mr. Vega trying to save Jaden that I barely feel my phone when it vibrates in my pocket. It's a call from Mom. *Crap.* She's probably worried sick. I should've called her immediately after all of this started, but I got caught up in this whirlwind of craziness and forgot. I answer the call and walk down the dark hallway, away from Mr. Vega, Jaden, and Trevor.

"Hey mom. I was just about to call you," I lie. "Have you seen what's going on in LA?" I don't want to freak her out about Jaden. Not until I'm absolutely sure that I'm in danger. Maybe he just had some kind of freak allergic reaction, a really severe one.

"It's not just happening in LA, sweetie. Have you looked

outside since you've been at work? It's happening here too. I don't want to scare you, but it doesn't look good over here. We've had about fifty people come into the hospital with the weird red rain all over them. None of them have shown any signs of turning into those things like in LA, but we have them all in quarantine just in case. On the news, they said that they're not even one hundred percent certain that the rain has any connection to the creatures. I just called to let you know that I'm okay and not to worry about me." She sounds confident, with no presence of fear in her unwavering voice.

"Mom, you have to get out of there. Did you see that video of the lady getting ripped out of the back of that taxi on CNN's website? Whatever those things are, they're dangerous. It tore the door off of the car like it was an orange peel. If there are fifty of them in the building, no quarantine will hold them back. Get out of there right now." I say, my voice cracking when I picture Mom screaming for her life surrounded by a group of those things.

"Calm down. I already have my stuff packed up and ready to go at the first sign of danger. The weird thing is, more than half of these patients are in liver failure. We're giving them blood transfusions right now, but we don't have nearly enough blood to supply everyone, especially if more people come in. I'm trying to do the best I can to help as many people as possible, Miles. Plus, it's still raining over here so I couldn't leave right now even if I wanted to," she says in a hushed voice, as if she doesn't want to be overheard as she tells me this new information about the liver failure. I don't like the thought of fifty ticking time bombs all around her, but I also don't want her to run out into the rain and become one herself. I can only hope that if anyone starts to change, the rain will have stopped by then and she can make a safe escape to her car.

"Be careful. I will lose my mind if something happens to you, Mom. Promise me you'll leave as soon as the rain lets up."

"I promise. I have to go now, Miles. There are people who need my help. I love you."

"I love you too. See you later." I end the call and turn around to go back by auditorium four.

"AAAAH!" A screech rips through the silent hallway. Seconds later, something heavy smashes into me and I spiral to the floor. I gasp and sit back up.

"Trevor, what was that?" I scream down the hall. He doesn't reply. I squint my eyes since I can barely see anything through this overwhelming darkness. Two figures lie on the floor exactly where I left Trevor, Mr. Vega, and Jaden. One of them has disappeared, but I can't tell who it is from right here. Someone to the right of me groans and I realize that I was just knocked down by a person, not an object. The phone call with Mom used up the last of my battery so I have absolutely no way to safely figure out who landed next to me without the flashlight.

I slowly stand up and take a few steps toward the dark, groaning figure on the floor. The person wears black clothes so I'm able to narrow it down to either Trevor or Jaden since Mr. Vega wears a green button-down dress shirt under his tan suit jacket. "Jaden? Trevor? Are you okay?" I whisper. The person lies on their stomach, face planted deeply into the dirty carpet. I can't even make out the color of their hair. I kneel down to flip the person over just as the lights flicker back on.

The numbers above the auditoriums turn back on, as solid white lights at first and then begin to flash every few seconds like they normally do. The hallway lights come back on next, which lessens the intensity of the darkness.

The person who crashed into me is Jaden. I identify him by his dark hair and sticky, damp clothes. I take a few steps back when I realize that it's him. I'm no detective, but someone who was just on the verge of death should not have enough strength to walk, let alone use enough force to knock me to the floor in a matter of minutes. Now that I know the groaning figure is Jaden, I'm still too skeptical to get anywhere near him, so I decide to walk over and figure out why Trevor and Mr. Vega are unconscious.

Drools spills from their open mouths much like Mr. Panderson this morning, which seems like it was a century ago. "Trevor." I tap my foot against his shin, which makes him kick his leg. He rolls over and ends up right on top of Mr. Vega's right hand. I lean down and shake him. After about the fourth of fifth shake, his eyes flutter open. I snap my fingers in front of his face. "Earth to Trevor. Is getting knocked out contagious today?" He groans, sits up on his elbows, and doesn't even attempt to stand up yet.

"I don't know. One minute I'm standing here watching Mr. V give CPR and the next I'm dreaming about chili cheese dogs and pepperoni pizza," he says. So that explains the lake of drool. He turns his head from side to side. "Where *is* Jaden anyway? He was lying right here." He pats the empty, open space to the right of him. Mr. Vega snores softly to his left.

I point down the hallway to the slumped figure on the floor. "Something crashed into my back and knocked me to the floor when I walked away to talk to my mom on the phone. When the lights came back on, I saw that it was him," I say. Trevor's face goes blank and he jumps to his feet.

"What if he's about to turn into one of those things? There's no possible way that he went from being on his deathbed to having enough energy to move all the way over there on his own." He leans down and gently places a hand on the snoozing Mr. Vega. "Mr. V, wake up. We have a problem," he whispers into the man's ear and steals nervous glances down the hall at Jaden. I suddenly realize just how exposed we are in this empty hallway. If Jaden turns right now, we're the only visible targets. Fresh meat.

I lean down next to Trevor, put my hand on Mr. Vega's other shoulder, and hope that the extra push will make him wake up faster. Seconds after my fingers make contact with his bony shoulder, he sits straight up and gasps. When he awakens out of nowhere, it gives me no time to lean backwards out of his way and his shiny, bald head smashes right into the bottom of my chin. I bite down on my tongue and the familiar metallic taste of blood fills my mouth.

"Ouch!" I scream out more as a reflex than anything else. The real pain doesn't hit until a few seconds later, so intense that tears form in my eyes.

Someone pinches me on my right arm. I wipe away the tears from my eyes with the back of my hand and find Trevor's fingers grasped onto my skin. He holds one finger up to his mouth to shush me and motions with his eyes down the hall at Jaden. Mr. Vega looks around, clearly confused. He tries to speak, but Trevor stops him with a hushed whisper.

"Look," he says.

A sharp black spike grows from the center of Jaden's back and rises a couple of inches every few seconds. It looks to be around four feet tall and about six inches thick. He still lies on his stomach. The wet spike glistens underneath the fluorescent lights and stands tall like a mountain peak. Since his face is hidden in the carpet, I can't tell if he's conscious or not, but I swear it sounds like he sobs softly into the floor. We stare in silence, too scared to make any sudden movements.

After about thirty seconds, the initial shock tapers off and Mr. Vega stands up. We tiptoe around the corner, out of Jaden's direct line of vision if he were to look this way, and huddle up close together.

"What should we do?" I ask in an urgent whisper. Part of me wants to run straight out of the exit door in auditorium four, but part of me also wants to go help evacuate customers from the building. I think back to the toothless little girl who spilled the popcorn earlier and decide that I'd rather die trying to save people than run out of the back door like a wimp.

"The proper procedure in emergency situations such as these is to go around and try to save as many people as possible. I'll go to inform the customers in number four about the situation. Trevor, stand watch over Jaden. Miles, go evacuate customers. Grab Ella on the way over to the other side and get her to help you," Mr. Vega says with much authority, as if it's an executive order and we don't have a choice if we want to keep our jobs. I glance over at Trevor and try to read his body language before I speak.

"Got it. I'll get people out of here," I say

"What should I do while I watch Jaden though?" Trevor asks in a shaky voice. He sounds terrified. I would be too if my task involved having to stand directly in the danger zone.

"Keep your distance. I'll call the police, but I'd say our best option is to pray that his condition doesn't progress any further. Not until everyone is out of the building. I trust you guys. This is potentially a real emergency. I'll come right behind you two after I inform the people in number four." With a nod, he turns around and walks over to number four. He pulls the door open slowly so it doesn't squeak or make any kind of noise and then he slips inside.

With Mr. Vega out of earshot, Trevor shouts at me in a whispered voice, "Are you out of your mind? Why would you agree to something like that? We have to get out of here," he says, doing his best to keep his voice low, but still firm.

"So you want to leave innocent people for dead? Maybe if I didn't have to waste time convincing you to go after Jaden earlier, we wouldn't be in this situation in the first place." I turn away from him before I lose control as my voice rises, which could get both of us killed.

"So all of this is my fault? Screw you, Miles," he angrily whispers behind me as I round the corner down the hallway that leads to the other side of the building. Jaden still lies in the same spot. It doesn't look like he's moved a single inch.

I walk as closely to the wall as I possibly can, away from my unconscious coworker. For the first time ever, I'm thankful for the nasty carpet since it absorbs every squeak that my shoes make. When I'm a safe enough distance away from Jaden, I pull myself away from the wall and move into the center of the hallway. Ella stands in the middle of the lobby directly in front of me, away from the podium where she tears tickets. When I reach the edge of the lobby, I call out to her in a voice that's loud enough for her to hear, but not loud enough to draw unwanted attention from behind me down the hall.

"Ella, come here. Mr. Vega says that you can leave the lobby. We have a bit of an emergency." She jogs over to me, with the green-paged book still in her hands.

"What's going on?" I fill her in on everything that has happened in the past hour. I begin with what Trevor saw behind the building, then move on to the CNN video on the tall man's phone, and then lead all the way up to the Royal Cinema's very own human Eiffel Tower. By the time I finish, she shivers as if she's in a blizzard.

"I wondered why no one had come into the building in a while. I could see that it was still raining, but I couldn't tell that it was red because it's too dark outside. So what exactly do you want me to do?" she asks in a panicky voice. She's a nervous wreck. I can't send her anywhere near Jaden. It would lead to an absolute disaster if he were to wake up in a violent state.

"Go into every theater on the other side and turn on the cleaning lights. People will be confused, but just go up to everyone, calmly explain what's going on, and tell them that they have to exit the auditorium immediately because it's not safe to be watching movies right now. If they ask for a refund or something, just tell them to call up here tomorrow because Mr. Vega didn't give me any guest passes to hand out. Most importantly, try not to let your nerves get the best of you. We don't want to create a stampede," I explain and she nods, her crystal blue eyes filled with fear.

"I'm gonna go get started on this side. Come and find me if you need anything, but be extremely quiet if you have to go anywhere near Jaden. Mr. Vega told Trevor to watch over him right now." I point behind me at Trevor, who leans against a wall at a very safe distance away from Jaden.

Ella gulps and takes a deep breath. "I can do this," she says before she turns away from me and walks through the lobby to the other side, almost at a run. I walk back toward Trevor just as Mr. Vega leads a group of people out of auditorium four. Mr. Vega motions for Trevor to come toward him.

When Trevor reaches him, he whispers something into his ear. Trevor immediately turns around and creeps past Jaden. He runs full speed toward me when he's far enough ahead not to possibly wake him up. He's out of breath by the time he reaches me.

"We…have…another…problem," he says between gasps of air. "The rain…hasn't stopped." My blood turns cold. If Jaden grows more of those spikes and wakes up as one of those things, we're trapped in here. Our only options are to stay inside and be torn apart or to risk going outside and turning exactly like him. If we stay inside, we won't be able to run from him if he's anywhere near as fast and powerful as the one from the video in LA.

"Well, this isn't good at all. What does Mr. Vega think we should do now?" I ask.

"None of the people that were in auditorium four want to leave right now. Who would? Especially when there's live proof right in front of them that this isn't all bullshit that the media is blowing out of proportion," he says. I look over his shoulder at Mr. Vega's group. The first thing that I notice is the sea of gray hair. They're elderly. Vulnerable. Easy targets.

"Well they should stay in here, but definitely not right where they are right now," I say.

"Mr. Vega wants us to clear out the rest of the theaters and gather everyone that wants to stay together in the lobby. After everyone is together, he wants to bring everyone upstairs and build a barricade until help arrives." Sounds like the best plan to me. I can't think of anything better.

"That's pretty smart. I have to go and warn Ella to not let people step outside. I sent her over to the other side to empty out the auditoriums," I say, spinning around to stop her from sending people to their doom.

"You should probably just stay over there with her and help speed up the process to get everyone out. Mr. V and I can finish up this side and then our groups can meet up before we go upstairs." He turns around to go back in the direction that he came from, but stops after he takes a few steps. "Oh, and don't think I'm not mad at you for leaving me to possibly die at the hands of Jaden. This is just really serious and I decided to be civil." He throws a glare over his shoulder and walks away.

I enter the eerily empty lobby and glance out of the front glass doors as I pass. Trevor didn't lie. The rain pelts the ground outside. I can't make out if it's still red, but I'm not about to go outside and find out. I turn away from the glass, which is now foggy from my breath.

The section of the building that I told Ella to clear out only has five auditoriums instead of eight like on the other side. It makes for a really awkwardly shaped building, but in this case, at least we have fewer customers to worry about on this side. Ahead of me, Ella talks to a family right outside of number ten. I pick up the pace as I get closer to them. Before I even say a word, the father's facial expressions let me know that they are already well aware of the situation. Ella nervously runs her hands through her hair. She turns to face me with swollen eyes when I walk up.

"So I assume that you've already seen what our next problem is?" I ask her.

"Yeah. So far, I've only made it into two theaters. Number nine was completely empty and these were the only people inside of number ten," she motions to the people right next to her, "Meet the Rodriguez family." A mom, a dad, and two scared little boys. The smaller of the two boys, probably around three or four, clutches onto his mom's leg with one hand and a stuffed puppy with the other.

"Hi. I'm Cesar and this is my wife, Marisela. These are our sons Jaime and little Julio," the dad says. When Julio hears his name, he waddles away from his mom's side to his dad, who scoops him up and bounces him up and down. Mr. Rodriguez extends his hand for me to shake it. I wipe my moist palm on my pants leg as discreetly as I can before I grab it.

"Miles," I say as I grip his hand. I feel terrible for them. A family comes out to spend some time together and now they're basically prisoners.

"Nice to meet you. This is all very scary. Ella tells us that one of those creatures is inside of the building somewhere. Is there a safe place that I can bring my family to?" he asks. People from Mr. Vega's group have started to silently trickle into the lobby. We need to speed up this whole evacuation process so we can go and join them.

"Yes sir," I point to the small group of people, "We're clearing out all of the auditoriums and then everyone that wants to can come upstairs until the rain stops. Please try to keep the children as quiet as possible. Jaden is unconscious right now and we don't want to wake him up,"

"Jaden?" Mrs. Rodriguez asks. Confusion washes over her beautiful face.

"Um, the creature you just referred to. He's a guy that works here. You can go ahead and join the people in the lobby while Ella and I check out the rest of the auditoriums," I say with a forced smile. It doesn't feel right to call Jaden a "creature." I'm still holding on to a sliver of hope that he isn't a complete lost cause and that it's somehow possible for us to save him. Mr. and Mrs. Rodriguez thank Ella and I before they walk away, as they try their best to keep the anxious children under control.

"Did they almost walk out into the rain?" I ask Ella when they're out of earshot.

"It was almost terrible. The dad actually walked out of the exit door inside of the auditorium, but luckily the spot was covered so he didn't get any of the rain on him," she says.

"Good thing. Let's hurry up and clear out these theaters so we can get upstairs. Being down here with Jaden gives me the creeps. I can't stop thinking about that video from LA. Whatever this is, it isn't good at all," I say.

"Miles," she calls out to me as I walk away from her to check the other auditoriums.

"What?" I quickly respond. We have zero time for small talk right now.

"I'm really scared. Why is the rain red? Why is there a spike on Jaden's back? I tried to look up some answers, but my phone has no service. My phone always has service. I'm with Verizon," she says, a million words a second flying out of her mouth. I have to use every ounce of my self-control to not roll my eyes at her.

"I don't know, Ella. Right now, we have to get these people out of their movies. We can figure it out when we go upstairs. I'll take numbers twelve and thirteen. You check eleven. If there's no one inside of there, just go back to the lobby and tell Mr. Vega that I'm on my way." She nods at me and goes to number eleven.

On the way to number twelve, I pull out my own phone to see if I have service. I press the home button several times to light up the screen, but it remains black. Shit. I forgot that I used the last of my battery to answer Mom's call. Of course I would forget to grab my charger on the day that I need it the most. I bet I'll have at least ten voicemails from Mom when I turn it back on.

I open the door to number twelve, the auditorium where the newest superhero movie plays. I walk over to the wall and flip on the cleaning lights, which feels so weird since we're usually not allowed to turn them on at all while the movies play, not even during the credits at the very end.

I make my way up the flat ramp that leads to the seating area and glance up into the audience. Four teenagers are on the very top row and a middle-aged couple sits right in the very center of the auditorium. Everyone stares down at me with puzzled looks on their faces. The movie is on a ridiculously loud scene so I have to actually go up and talk to everyone individually instead of just making one big announcement down at the bottom of the stairs. First, I go up to the couple in the middle.

"Excuse me," I shout over the loud explosions and gunfire, "We have an emergency situation. Please wait at the bottom of the stairs until I get those kids from the top."

The couple is nicely dressed, way too fancy to be inside of a dark theater. The dark haired lady is closest to me and can hear me the most, so she nods and turns to whisper something into her date's ear. They gather up their popcorn and drinks and descend down the stairs. As they pass me, a sickly sweet mixture of perfume and cologne fills the air.

Before I go up to talk to the teenagers, I make sure they stop at the bottom and don't try to leave out. When they reach the bottom step, they stop and talk to each other, while glancing up in my direction. I continue up the stairs until I reach the top.

"Hey guys. We have a problem. I need y'all to come with me," I say to the girl that sits at the very edge of the aisle. She rolls her eyes at me. She has long, black braids with streaks of red and purple mixed in and wears shorts that are nearly nonexistent. The guy next to her has piercing green eyes and spiky blonde hair. His hand sits on her lap, so I assume that they're dating. The two girls that sit next to them are identical twins; one wears a Lady Gaga concert T-shirt and the other a pink and white striped blouse. They're all probably either juniors or seniors in high school, but Briskwood High is small enough to know everyone and I'm confident that I've never seen them before in my life.

"Do we really have to leave?" The girl with the braids asks loudly. Even over the movie, her strong New Orleans accent is evident.

"Yes, it's an emergency," I shout back to her. She leans down to pick her purse up from the floor and peels her boyfriend's hand off of her lap. I'm glad this happened during the week. If all of this went down on the weekend, the building would definitely be filled with even more stubborn teenagers.

I let all of them go down first, ahead of me. The twins are short and pudgy. It takes them a little longer to get down the stairs so I'm stuck behind them, left to impatiently tap my fingers on the railing as I wait to lower myself to the next step. This is the worst time to be stuck behind slow movers since every second counts right now.

By the time we reach the ground floor, the movie is at a part that has less action, so I'm able to speak in a voice that's slightly lower than a yell. "I'm not sure if y'all are aware of what's going on in LA right now, but the same thing is happening here," I say just as Captain America calls for the Avengers to assemble on the giant looming screen behind us. I wish they were here to protect all of us from whatever these creatures are. "Red rain fell from the sky and turned people into these freaky mutant things that are super strong and grow black spikes all over their bodies. We have a person inside of the building with us right now that is in the process of changing into one of them and we can't leave because it's still raining."

The dark haired lady's mouth falls open. "So what are we supposed to do? Where is the person that's changing right now?" she asks.

"He's currently unconscious. After all of the auditoriums are empty, my manager will bring anyone who wants to stay upstairs where it's more secure." As soon as the words are out of my mouth, the girl with braids breaks away from her boyfriend's side and gets right in my face.

"So why are you standing here telling us about all of this in a place that isn't safe? Let's MOVE!" she shouts, turning from me and walking away, almost at a jog, to the entrance where I just came in. We follow behind her, with me in the front, the couple and the boyfriend in the middle, and the twins trailing along at the end. I can tell that she's going to be a problem.

"Hey." I call after her, but it's too late. She's already made it into the hallway. I continue to lead the group toward the entrance.

"I'm sorry about her. She tends to overreact and stop thinking when she gets scared." The smell of tobacco and mint gum fills my nose. I keep walking, but glance over my shoulder and see that the girl's boyfriend talks directly into my ear. She better learn how to control herself or she won't last long at all in this potentially dangerous situation.

When we leave out of the auditorium, she's already halfway up the hallway headed to the lobby. "Amalia!" the boyfriend screams after her, "Slow down, you might run right to your death." She spins around and stops right in her tracks. After a few seconds, she starts to walk back toward the rest of the group.

"Sorry, but I'm not gonna stand around and wait to be killed. We need to hurry," she says when she rejoins the rest of us.

"You don't even have all of the details. You're going to get yourself killed one of these days if you don't stop to think before you act. Let's stick with this guy, he seems like he knows what he's doing." the boyfriend says. She opens her mouth to respond, but I cut in before she can start an argument.

"As much as I would love to stand here and listen to this all night, I think we have more important things to worry about right now," I say sarcastically. One of the twins nods her head in agreement. At least one of the people in this group has a functioning brain.

The well-dressed, middle-aged man is the next to speak. "If you don't mind, my wife and I would like to go ahead and join the rest of the group that's headed upstairs. Where did you say that we need to meet at again?"

I point down the hallway. "In the lobby. If y'all want to head down there, that's fine. I only have two more auditoriums to check until I'm finished," I say, happy to have less customers to worry about. The man glances at his wife, who isn't paying attention and is more focused on repeatedly pressing a button on her phone.

"It doesn't work," she says in voice that comes out high-pitched and squeaky, "It says I have no service." Ella re-emerges from the auditorium right next to where we stand.

"Ella, did your phone start to work again? This lady doesn't have service either," I say. She holds her phone to where I can see the screen as she walks up. A big red X pops up every time she presses the green button to call someone.

"Nope. Does yours work?" She asks.

"It was earlier, but I'm not sure. It's dead. Was there anyone in number eleven?" I ask.

"No, it was completely empty. I'm about to head back to the lobby to join the group. I'll see you in a few." She walks away. I turn back to face my own group.

"We're gonna follow behind her and join the larger group now. Thanks for your help," the man says once he sees that he has my attention again. The lady still tries to get her phone to work as they turn away from us. She looks totally ridiculous as she holds it up above her head trying to catch a signal.

The girl with braids, Amalia, clears her throat loudly. "So, this whole not dying a terrible death thing. Let's get to it. Chop chop," she says, clapping her hands together. Even though she's rude, she's right. Jaden is a ticking time bomb and I want to be nowhere near him when he explodes.

"Okay. Just wait right here while I check this last auditorium. Don't do anything stupid like run off into the rain while I'm gone," I say to them. Amalia rolls her eyes while the twins and boyfriend laugh.

I walk away from them and enter auditorium thirteen. I scan the rows of seats and see no customers. The only sign that there were even people in here today are the few cups and popcorn tubs that were left behind from the earlier showing that Trevor and I didn't get to clean. We would be in serious trouble if we left an auditorium dirty on a regular day, which it most definitely is not. I turn around and walk back into the hallway alone since there's no one to add to my small group of customers.

The twins sit on the floor right outside of the auditorium. Amalia and her boyfriend stand off to the side of them, quietly talking to each other. They stop when I walk over to them.

"Ready to go now?" the boyfriend asks. He looks like he'll beat me down to the ground if I say anything other than yes. I'm not sure why he has an attitude, when he could've just gone with the other couple a few minutes ago.

"Yep. There was no one inside the theater," I say. The twins stand up and walk over to the three of us.

"Fantastic," Amalia says with a sarcastic smile. I walk down the hall toward the lobby and they follow closely behind me.

"Hey, I never got your name. I'm Spencer. This is Amalia, my girlfriend. These two are my sisters, Salem and Scarlett. We're triplets," he says, which catches me off guard. I never even considered that they might be triplets. Spencer is taller and thinner than both of the girls.

"I'm Miles," I say without turning around to look at him. A medium sized group of about forty people have gathered together in the center of the lobby. Most of them must have come from Trevor and Mr. Vega's group since Ella and I only found about ten people on this side. It's pretty impressive that so many people were able to evacuate from that side of the building without disturbing Jaden. At least, I assume he's still unconscious since no one screams and runs for their lives.

"So what do we do once we get upstairs?" A voice that I don't recognize asks. I glance over my shoulder and see that it's either Scarlett or Salem, whichever one wears the black concert shirt.

"We wait. My manager has already called the police, but they probably can't do anything until the rain lets up." I'm dying to know what's being said on the news right now. I wonder if this is only happening here and in LA or if the unnatural rain is also pummeling the other cities that had severe weather earlier too.

"What does the monster or whatever look like? This has to be a joke. Rain doesn't turn people into... killers." She struggles to find a word to describe what the people have turned into. She tries to continue, but her sister slaps her on the arm and interrupts.

"Salem, don't be ridiculous. You have no idea what's going on and saying that it's a joke won't help anything," the sister in the pink and white blouse says. So Salem wears the Lady Gaga shirt and Scarlett wears the blouse. Got it. The look on Salem's face tells me that she's used to getting shut down by her sister.

"Fine. Don't say anything when it turns out that I'm right and this is all bullshit," Salem says. We reach the lobby just as I realize that I'd rather have Jaden rip me apart than to spend another second around these people.

"Y'all can join in at the back of the group," I point to where a few people stand around talking, "I'm gonna go and find my manager." I leave them and slowly make my way through the group of people to get to the front. Mr. Vega is too short to speak directly to the crowd, so he stands on a bench and towers over everyone. It thunders yet again, slightly softer this time.

When he spots me coming through the crowd, his face wrinkles up into a frown. Trevor, Ella, and Simon, the guy who must have taken over inside the box office when Marchelle got off earlier, all stand on the floor right next to Mr. Vega.

"It's about time you showed up," he snaps at me when I walk over and stand next to Trevor, who's still mad about me agreeing to help save lives and doesn't even acknowledge my presence.

"Sorry. I told him you were right behind me, but he took it too literally," Ella whispers to me.

"Attention, customers of Royal Cinema. Now that everyone has joined us," he pauses to glare in my direction, "We can begin the process of bringing everyone upstairs where it'll be safer until the police arrive. Please try to remain calm. We don't want to draw any unnecessary attention this way."

A baby cries loudly from the center of the group. The people that stand at the front of the group turn around to look. Trevor nervously glances over his shoulder at the knocked out Jaden. Otherwise, the hall is deserted and still.

"Why is there nobody watching over him right now?" I ask.

"Maybe because it's extremely dangerous and we have no idea what's even going on? Why don't you go do it since you're so concerned?" He says with a growl.

"The attitude isn't necessary. I was just wondering," I say.

"You didn't speak up when—" he starts to say. Someone from the crowd suddenly screams out, a balding man who stands near the front. His arm is outstretched, pointing behind the bench where Mr. Vega tries to give his speech. My back faces whatever is going on so I have to spin around and then squint down the hall.

At first, it looks like nothing has changed. I have to use every muscle in my eyes to see what has caused an urgent whisper to spread through the crowd, growing louder and louder by the second. Another spike slowly rises out of Jaden's back, growing out diagonally from the first one. From right here, it looks like it's a little longer than the one that sticks straight up. This time, a piece of his shirt has ripped free and hangs limply from the tip of the spike like a black flag. I feel a slight push on my back as the crowd carefully inches forward to get a better look.

"Everyone remain calm," Mr. Vega says again, surrounded by a sea of people that crowd around the bench. "We need to get upstairs NOW! Trevor, put in the code to the door and hold it open until everyone is in. I'll unlock the elevator and bring people up that way too," he says as he looks down and speaks directly to us, the employees.

The curious customers are a few feet down the hall, still a safe distance away from Jaden, but if he were to awaken right now, it would be an absolute bloodbath. Trevor pushes his way through the mass of bodies and puts in the code to the door that leads to the stairs.

"Miles and Simon, direct these people. Ella, grab my keys and run upstairs to open the door to the projection booth. Stay up there and line everyone up against the wall so we can get a headcount. And don't let anyone touch the projectors." He tosses the ring of keys at Ella, who catches them and races through the doorway to the stairs.

I go to the front of the crowd and show people where they need to go. "It's time for everyone to move upstairs where it'll be safe. To your left, the door that leads to the staircase is open and a few people can go up the elevator too," I say in a loud voice so I can be heard over the whispering of the crowd that collects into a roar. Mr. Vega has jumped down from the bench and is now at the elevator to put in the code to unlock it. From the center of the group, the Rodriguez family silently slips over to wait for the elevator to open.

People barely pay attention to me, as they mindlessly stare down the hall at Jaden lying on the floor. I clap three times as an attempt to snap them out of their trance, which causes the people closest to me to jump and then glare in my direction. "Now that I have your attention," I jab my thumb in the direction of the staircase. People reluctantly make their way to the staircase and bump into each other because they're still more focused on staring at the danger than trying to get away from it.

Now that people at the front have started to move, the rest of them follow, and the crowd shrinks down to half the original size in about a minute. Amalia and the triplets hang around by the elevator, waiting for it to come back down. I notice that Salem and Scarlett don't talk to each other and I can imagine that Scarlett has already taken the opportunity to rub it in her sister's face that she was right.

I scan the faces of the few remaining people and that's when I see him. The man who kicked me over the railing stands off to the side by himself, still wearing the dark green baseball cap. He must have mixed in with the crowd because I didn't notice him until now. Anger takes over my body and I feel my face turn hot with rage.

"Hey!" I yell and push past the remaining people, who immediately walk to the stairs when they see how mad I am, until I stand in front of him. His eyes nervously dart from side to side, just like earlier.

"Why did you—" I start, but he doesn't listen to me. We make eye contact for a split second and then he takes off down the hall toward Jaden. I run after him, completely forgetting about just how dangerous the situation is. He stops when he stands right next to Jaden and reaches for something under his shirt. At first, I think he's about to take his phone out of his pocket to take picture.

"NOOOOO!" I scream at the top of my lungs when I realize what he's actually about to do.

Under his bulky shirt, he has hidden a gun. He jerks it free and holds it directly over Jaden's unmoving head.

Then, he pulls the trigger three times.

CHAPTER 6

I'm able to stumble a few steps back toward the lobby before my legs give out and send me spiraling to the floor. When I fall down, my head smacks into the floor and leaves me staring at the wall. Stars fill my vision and swirl around like they're chasing after each other in a game of tag. I don't move from the spot where I lie and for a moment, I think I'm going to lose consciousness for the second time today, both caused by the same psychotic man. My ears ring from the gunshots and I don't hear my name being called until Amalia's long, brown legs tower over me.

"Miles." I read Amalia's lips before she grabs me by my arm and hauls me up to my feet effortlessly. She shouts something, but it sounds muffled because of my messed up ears. She drags me along the hall, with the help of Spencer, who I didn't notice at first. Up ahead, Trevor still holds the door to the staircase open, waving his arms frantically to tell us that we need to hurry up.

Amalia and Spencer shove me inside and slam the door shut behind them, but not before I turn my head around to steal a quick look down the hall at the grisly scene. The man sits on the floor next to Jaden's lifeless body. I can't tell if he still holds the murder weapon, but he rocks back and forth as if he's in a trance. It's the last thing I see before I land with a thud on the bottom of the staircase.

I try to stand up, but my vision goes black and I slump back down. I'm able to hear Trevor's voice a little better than when Amalia shouted in my ear at close range and realize that my hearing is slowly, but surely returning back to normal. "He just walked over there and murdered him. Blew his brains out," Trevor says. I blink the dizzying blackness out of my eyes just in time to see him punch the wall and then scrunch his face up in pain. He massages his hand and then sits next to me on the bottom step.

"I was wrong earlier," he says, "This is all not going to blow over by tomorrow." He's right. At the very least, we'll probably be dragged into court as witnesses because of what we just saw. This isn't a situation like the whole Mr. Panderson thing where there is still a lot of speculation about what happened. This was cold-blooded murder and all of us saw it go down. Before today, I had never seen a dead body in person and now I've seen two. Hell, at the rate today is going, the world might be over by tomorrow and we won't have to worry about court.

I look up at the wall where a clock hangs above the staircase and see that it's just after 11:00, the time I was supposed to get off. I feel guilty. If I would've gone home after I took the fall instead of being money hungry, I wouldn't have been here to confront the man and Jaden might not be dead right now. I can't believe how much has happened in just a couple of hours.

"Can we go upstairs and join everyone else?" Amalia asks softly, which interrupts my dark, over-analytical thoughts. "I don't feel safe right by this door with that maniac on the loose out there." Her voice has lost much of the edge that it had when I first met her. Spencer has a protective arm wrapped around her, gently rocking her back and forth. I can tell that she's on the verge of having a breakdown. Scarlett and Salem quietly sob together as they stare down at the white tile floor.

"Yeah. Let's go," I say. I stand more slowly this time so my vision doesn't go black and ascend the long staircase, with the others following closely behind me.

When we reach the top of the staircase, the doors that lead to the projection booth, our new safe haven, and the break room are both locked shut. Great. Mr. Vega probably thinks that everyone has already made it up here, so Ella doesn't hold the door open anymore. I don't have the key to get inside and I also feel like bursting in would further scare a ton of people that are already on edge. I tap my knuckles on the hard, metal door three times. Hopefully, they haven't started to build a barricade yet.

"Who is it?" Mr. Vega's voice answers my knock. He tries to be stern, but he just sounds like a ten-year-old standing up to a bully on the playground.

"It's Miles. I'm with Trevor and a few customers," I say. He cracks open the door just enough so that he can peek out with one eye, most likely to check and make sure that we don't have any unwelcome surprises with us. When he's satisfied with what he sees, he opens the door and steps aside to allow us in.

Inside, the usually dark and gloomy projection booth is lit up and full of life. Customers sit along the wall to our right and stare up at us as we walk in. Two little boys play in the open space between the huge projectors that run auditoriums five and six, tossing a bouncy ball back and forth. One of the boys throws the ball too hard and causes it to bounce into projector five, which it ricochets off of and then flies down the hallway. The kids run after it, nearly crashing into me as they pass by.

"Be careful, those projectors are expensive!" Mr. Vega shouts after them.

Ella walks up and down the line with a pad of paper and a pen to count how many people were unfortunate enough to be in the building when all of this started. (Or very fortunate depending on how you look at it. This is a pretty safe spot, situated on the second floor behind two passcode-protected doors.)

"Are y'all the last people left to come up? I want to move something in front of the door just in case." Mr. Vega points to the large black filing cabinet that is pushed up against the wall right next to the door.

"I have to tell you something important," I say and drag him away from where the customers sit. Trevor goes in the opposite direction, talking with Amalia and the triplets. They check in with Ella, who scribbles something onto her pad, before they plop down at the end of the long line.

"What's going on?" he asks when we're far enough away so that none of the customers can hear us.

"Jaden is dead. The man who kicked me over the railing in Mad Max earlier is still inside the building," I swallow and take a deep breath when my throat starts to close up, "I guess he must've snuck into another movie after he knocked me out. He was mixed in with the people that we brought up here and I didn't notice him until almost everyone else was out of the lobby. When I went up to confront him, he ran away from me to where Jaden was lying on the floor, pulled a gun out, and shot him three times in the head," my voice cracks. Mr. Vega is stunned into silence and his bulging eyes threaten to pop out of his head. He's so pale that I'm scared he's going to collapse.

"What?" He shouts after a few seconds, but I quickly put a finger to my lips and point behind him at the customers at the front of the line that stare up at us as we talk. The last thing we need is for a rumor to travel down the line of nervous people, getting more and more distorted the farther it goes.

"Is the man still down there? Did he try to shoot you too?" he asks in a much quieter voice.

"When I came up here, he was sitting on the floor, rocking back and forth next to Jaden's body. And no he didn't try to shoot me, but he could have because I was on the floor right next to where it happened. Two of the customers that came up here with Trevor and I saved my life." Amalia's blurry, terrified face suddenly pops into my head from when she helped me to my feet.

"This is not what I signed up for," he mutters under his breath. "Why were you lying on the floor?" he asks with a puzzled look on his face.

"I was so shocked by the gunshots that when I tried to run back to the lobby my legs gave out." It scares me to think that I was lying right next to the murderer, a sitting duck right in the crosshairs for him to finish what he attempted to do earlier when he kicked me over the railing.

"I'm going to call the police again. Maybe it's stopped raining over on their end." He pulls out his phone and dials 9-1-1, puts it up to his ear, and waits. After a few seconds, he frowns and pulls the phone away from his ear to look at the screen. "That's strange. It says I have no service. It worked just fine the last time I checked. Let me use yours."

I shake my head. "My phone is dead. Ella and another customer that tried to make a call had no service either." I'm sure that the red rain has something to do with this. There's no other reason why all of these phones would stop working at the same time.

"I'm going to ask everyone in the crowd if any of them have one that works," he says and then turns away from me to walk back to the line of customers. He stops at the very front and clears his throat.

"Does anyone have a phone that works right now? I need to make a call," he speaks loudly to be heard over the roar of the movie projectors. At first, his request is answered with silence. All along the line, people reach into purses and pockets to pull out their phones.

"I have no bars," a lady screams from the back.

"Me either," a man that sits right in front of where I stand yells back to her. This goes on for several minutes as almost everyone in the crowd confirms that none of their phones work. All of the lit up screens remind me of the only concert I've ever been to: Coldplay, when I was in the sixth grade.

Then, an unlikely hero comes to the rescue just as Mr. Vega is about to give up. An elderly lady with a cane stands up and slowly makes her way in our direction. She has one hand buried deep inside of her oversized purse, which has a miniature umbrella that is much too small to provide any protection from the deadly rain, sticking out of the top of it. She stops in front of Mr. Vega and pulls her hand out from the abyss of a purse. Her thin, bony fingers clutch a small silver flip phone.

"I was able to call my daughter who lives in New York a few minutes before we came up here. It's old and doesn't have Internet like those fancy ePhones, but it'll get the job done." She hands over the small device, which Mr. Vega eagerly grabs.

"Thank you so much, Ms. Suzanne. I'll bring it back to you once I'm done making the call," he says gratefully to the old lady. She smiles a sweet grandmotherly smile and turns around using the cane to direct herself back to where she sits. I wonder how Mr. Vega knows her name, but I figure that she must have been in that first group of people who were evacuated from auditorium four when she sinks back to the floor and disappears into a small group of elderly customers. Mr. Vega walks over to the secluded spot where I told him about what happened to Jaden, squinting at the small screen on the phone and keying in numbers.

With a sigh, I walk to rejoin Trevor and the others that sit along the wall. Before I'm even halfway there, Ella stops me right in front of the line of people and whispers in my ear, "What is going on? I saw you and Mr. Vega talking over there." I glance down and see several customers watching us intently, trying to grab onto bits and pieces from our conversation since they're totally in the dark right now. A man with long, shaggy hair makes eye contact with me and stands up to get in my face.

"Is there something that we're not being told? We're not blind. We see all of this cryptic whispering going on," he snarls at me. A few people enthusiastically scream "yeah!" and several heads nod in agreement. This isn't good. No one can know that someone was just gunned down in the building, even if it was someone who might've tried to kill us, or all hell will break loose.

"Sir, nothing is going on. We're all just a little on edge right now. None of us know anything that we haven't told you about already," I lie. The man looks me up and down like I've just deeply offended him, lets out an obnoxious snort, and then drops back down next to a grungy looking lady who scowls up at me.

I look away from them and my eyes land on the pad of paper in Ella's hand. She's drawn a chart that separates the number of customers from the number of employees in the building right now. She has made little tally marks on both sides of the chart, each standing for one person. On the employee side, there are six marks and a chill runs up my spine when I realize that she's included Jaden in the count. The customer side has way more tally marks and at the bottom of the page, she has written the number thirty-five for the grand total.

"The employee side is inaccurate. Don't include Jaden," I say, pointing to the chart and walking away without explaining myself before she starts to ask questions she really doesn't want the answers to. As I walk away, I realize that she also hasn't included the gunman either. She stares at me before she looks down to scratch her work out with a pen and recalculate the tally.

When I reach where Trevor has settled down against the wall with Amalia and the triplets, I sit down across from them in the middle of hall, cross-legged as if I'm still in elementary school. Amalia rests her head on Spencer's shoulder with her eyes closed. Her long, colorful braids hang just low enough to brush the top of the ice-cold tile floor. My shoes squeak when I sit down, which is loud enough to scare her out of her nap, revealing bloodshot eyes. Spencer sits straight up and massages the spot where her head was, which is slightly damp from either tears or drool. Scarlett is stretched out on the floor, tracing the words 'HELP ME' that Trevor and I carved into the wall one day while we were bored, to support the ghost story that we tell to new employees.

Salem and Trevor talk about what sounds like an episode of The Walking Dead. I wonder if they realize that our own lives might soon make that show look like child's play.

"Spencer. Amalia. I never got the chance to say thank you for saving my ass earlier. I might not be here right now if it wasn't for you two," I reach out and awkwardly shake both of their hands.

"Well, it was Spencer's idea. I was just waiting for the elevator. If it would've come down in time, I would've jumped on there so fast and not looked back," Amalia says with a snark.

"Oh please. You ran down there to grab him before I could talk some sense into you about why it wasn't a good idea to run toward where a gun was just fired. It's okay to show that you have a heart," Spencer says. I cringe when he mentions the gun and look around to make sure that no one heard him.

"Hey, keep your voice down about the gun. Do you want to start a riot?" I whisper to him.

Scarlett suddenly sits up and inserts herself into the conversation. "It's true, Miles. Amalia ran to your rescue before any of us could process what had just happened. For some reason, she just wants everyone to believe that she's an uncaring, cold-hearted bitch." Amalia springs to her feet and bounds over Spencer's outstretched legs so that she stands directly over the smirking girl.

"Would you like to repeat what you just said?" She balls her hands up into fists. Trevor and Salem stop talking just long enough to see what all of the noise is about, and then go right back to their private conversation. He says something that I can't hear, but it makes her break into a fit of laughter.

"Nah, I'm good," she says, flattening her body back down onto the floor. She goes back to running her finger along the dusty wall.

Amalia returns to her seat just as Mr. Vega gets off the phone and brings it back to Ms. Suzanne. As soon as the phone is back in the old lady's hands, he goes back to the front of the line to make another announcement.

He claps his hands together twice to get the attention of the restless crowd. "The connection was spotty, but I was able to get in contact with the police and they said that the rainfall has significantly slowed down over on their end. They're about to layer up several officers in protective clothing and will be here to assess our situation shortly." He pauses until the cheering calms down. "If anyone has questions, you can direct them to one of the employees. They all have on shirts with a red, green, and black shield on the back." I'm the only person who doesn't sit up against the wall, so I scoot up next to Amalia and try to blend in with the crowd to avoid having to answer any ridiculous complaints.

"I'm about to walk around and shut down these projectors. Guest passes will be handed out once the police say that it's okay for us to go downstairs," he says, continuing his speech. At the mention of free passes, the cheering erupts once again, even louder this time. "Oh and if I'm not around when the officers get here, I told them to knock on the door four times in quick succession as kind of a secret code so we know it's them." He turns around and descends the small flight of stairs that lead to the projectors for auditoriums one through eight.

"I'm glad all of this is almost over. I need an uninterrupted nap," Amalia says as she lays her head back on Spencer's shoulder. I guess she still hasn't grasped onto the fact that this might not be an isolated event. The entire city could be filled with those creatures right now, and we have no way of knowing.

I can't even imagine sleeping. If I even close my eyes for a few seconds, I'll have to relive Jaden's death all over again. If

I were to actually fall asleep, I'm sure the nightmares would be the worst I've ever had in my life.

Just like I assumed earlier because of Amalia's accent and me never seeing them around school, Spencer confirms that they're not from around here. Amalia has dozed off again and snores softly when Spencer fills me in on their background. Trevor has stopped talking to Salem and sits next to me, listening closely.

"We're from New Orleans. Juniors, well technically seniors now, at Benjamin Franklin High School. We got out for summer break about a week ago and came to visit Amalia's grandmother, who has cancer. We brought her to the hospital for chemotherapy and decided to come watch a movie while we waited for her to get finished. Bad idea," he stops, drapes his hands over his knees, and lets out a deep sigh. Briskwood only has one hospital, the one where Mom works. I decide that it's best not to tell him about all of the red rain covered patients that were brought in.

"I figured y'all weren't from around here since I didn't remember ever seeing your faces around school before. You don't sound like you're from New Orleans though," I say, noticing that he doesn't have a strong accent like his girlfriend.

"Wasn't born there. My sisters and I are from Ohio. We moved to New Orleans four years ago when our dad got a new job, which is where I met Amalia in the seventh grade."

"Our dad made us come here with the two lovebirds so that he could have the house to himself with his girlfriend," Salem says with a sour look on her face, glaring at her brother resentfully. In the short amount of time that I've known all of them, I can already tell that the two identical sisters are closer to each other than to their brother.

"Don't look at me like that. You could've gone back to that church camp instead," Spencer says.

"You know I hate that place. I would rather be trapped up here in this smelly booth for the entire summer than to ever go back there," she says. Curiosity gets the best of me, so I decide to ask what could have been so terrible about the place.

"What's so bad about this church camp?" I ask as nonchalantly as I can, just in case she shoots me down and tells me to mind my own business.

"It's not something that we discuss," Scarlett chimes in before her sister can answer.

"Oh. Well, I was just curious. I've always known church camps to be a lot of fun," I say.

"Salem claims that she saw a perverted nun peeping at her through the shower curtain one night. I think it's total BS," Spencer says, which makes the mouths of both girls fall open.

"SPEN-CER! Why would you say that? I hate you so much!" Salem shrieks in a high-pitched voice, which not only causes Amalia to wake up, but to spring to her feet. She looks dazed and confused before her narrowed eyes lock onto the screaming girl. She moves toward Salem at lightning speed, accidentally bumps into me, and knocks me flat on my back. When she reaches Salem, she pins her up against the wall by the neck with one hand. The impact of Salem's head smacking into the wall causes her thick, red-framed glasses to clatter to the floor.

"I was up all night trying to tend to my sick, maybe dying, grandmother while your ass was snoring in the bed and you have the nerve to scream when I finally get a few minutes to rest?" Amalia screams, even louder than Salem. People stand up and gather around the scene Amalia is making, as if this is a fight in a high school cafeteria. I jump to my feet so the crowd doesn't engulf me.

Salem shakes like a leaf in a thunderstorm, or in this case, a bloodrainstorm. "But Spencer told—" she's immediately interrupted before she can explain herself.

"I didn't ask you what happened," Amalia growls. I wonder if she's always this cranky and extreme or if it's just from the lack of sleep. "You're already on thin ice for calling me an uncaring bitch. Watch it, girl."

"I didn't even say that, Scarlett did!" Salem exclaims in an exasperated voice. Amalia looks slightly embarrassed for a split second, but she quickly regains her tough composure.

"Well, you probably used twin telepathy or something to tell her to say that. You two basically share a brain anyway. I hear y'all whisper behind my back all the time. Usually, I just choose not to say anything." Amalia removes her arm from Salem, who immediately takes in deep gulps of air. Then, she angrily shoves her way through the crowd and descends down the small flight of stairs that Mr. Vega went down a few minutes ago. I stare after her and watch as she disappears around a corner.

"You know how she gets when she's under stress. Maybe you'll keep your voice down next time," Spencer says to his sister, who is still doubled over trying to catch her breath. I can't believe this guy, defending the girl who just choked his sister in front of him. He seems like the type of boy-friend that would try to defend his girlfriend while covered in the blood of someone she just murdered. I suddenly get the strongest urge to break his nose. Before I can act on this feeling, he turns away without another word to any of us and takes off after Amalia.

"Is he always that... protective of her?" Trevor asks with his eyebrows raised, struggling to find a word to describe the strange relationship.

"Yeah. Queen Amalia can do no wrong. Once, she rear-ended the back of a car because she was texting while driving and he tried to say it was because Salem and I were arguing and distracted her," Scarlett says, rolling her eyes.

"That's crazy," he says, shaking his head.

Salem stands up straight after she finally regains control of her breath. She reaches down to pick up her glasses from the floor and repositions them on her face. They tilt to the side and slide down the bridge of her nose, which makes her sigh.

"Are you okay?" I ask her.

"I'm fine. That girl needs some strong medication though," she says angrily, and then slides back down the wall to sit on the floor.

I'm not exactly sure how I feel about Amalia. On one hand, she is over the top and overreacts way too often, but it might just be her way to deal with a million different emotions because of her grandmother's cancer. Plus, one of her impulsive actions saved my life.

My grandfather had cancer a few years ago and it was pretty serious for a while. It was so bad that Mom had to use some vacation time at her job and go down to where my grandparents live in South Padre Island to help my grandmother take care of him. This left just my dad and I at home, but he was at work most of the time, so I mostly had to deal with all of my sad thoughts alone.

Mom would call to update us on his condition at least three times a week, usually after each radiation session. The

doctors thought he was going to lose his battle and even rec-
ommended that the family come to say our goodbyes. The
next week, they did some final X-rays before they stopped
the treatments and saw that there was significant shrinkage
in the tumors. They decided to continue with the radiation
sessions and about a month later, he was declared cancer
free and has been doing God knows what on his military job
ever since. I know I was very moody during the whole thing,
so I can definitely see where Amalia's anger comes from.
Actually, I'm sure she's even more stressed out than I was
because of the situation we're in right now.

I'm lost in thought when I realize that someone is calling
my name as they walk up behind me, emerging from the crowd
that has receded now that the Amalia show is over. When I turn
around, Mr. Rodriguez, one of the only customers that Ella
found earlier, stands in front of me. He holds his youngest son,
Julio. Sadly, his beautiful wife must have stayed behind with
their other son, whose name I can't remember.

"What can I do for you, sir?" I ask when I snap out of my
trance and remember that I work here. Julio stares at me
with his large, saucer sized eyes. The bowl cut hair outlines
his sharp features and makes him look like a little angel.

"My son here had an accident," Mr. Rodriguez says. I'm
so wired by the events of the day that my mind instantly jumps to the worst-case scenario, some kind of serious,
life-threatening accident, that I don't even notice the cloud
covered diaper bag that hangs off of his shoulder.

"What's the problem?" I ask, my eyes growing to the size
of little Julio's.

"Nothing major," he chuckles, noticing my sudden de-
fensiveness. "I just need to find a restroom to change Julio's
diaper. Is there one up here or are they all downstairs?"

"The one up here has been out of order for more than a year, but I can walk you to it and you can change him on the sink top. There should be plenty of room to lay him down and get him cleaned up," I say, using my fake interested in the customer voice. The booth is pretty much just a gigantic, empty corridor with glass windows on the walls that have projectors bolted down to the floor in front of them to play the movies for each auditorium. The restroom is located at the very end of the long hallway, right next to the projector for auditorium thirteen. I walk, with Mr. Rodriguez and Julio right by my side, in the opposite direction of where Mr. Vega just went.

I press a button on the back of each projector that I pass on my way to the restroom to turn them off since Mr. Vega hasn't made it down to this side yet. By the time we reach the restroom door at the end of the hallway, all of them are turned off. Now that the roar from the projectors doesn't fill the empty space, the only sound comes from the group that we just left, but they're so far away that it sounds like a muffled murmur.

I brush the thick spider webs off of the door handle and then open the door with an earsplitting creak. "Watch out for spiders," I say as I flip a switch on the wall that turns a single, dim light bulb on above my head.

A huge roach crawls around inside of the rusty sink, but disappears down the drain when we walk in. The toilet has no water in it and is equally as stained as the sink. I grab a roll of dusty paper towels that sit on the floor, rip a few off, and try to get as much of the dirt off of the sink top as I can before Mr. Rodriguez sets Julio down.

It's freezing in here; the air conditioning seems to be the only thing that still works in this deserted restroom. When

Julio touches the cold sink top, he lets out a small cry and squirms. "Shhh, you're okay," Mr. Rodriguez says in a calm voice and tries to get him to stay still.

"Do you want me to use the flashlight on your phone so you can have more light? I would use mine, but it's dead," I say.

"I left my phone back in the car on accident. This should be fine. I've changed so many diapers that I'm sure I could do it in my sleep," he laughs softly and then rips the used diaper off of Julio. The strong smell of urine washes over me and causes my eyes to water. I turn my head to the side and try to block out the smell, inhaling the musty air of the small restroom.

Mr. Rodriguez reaches inside the diaper bag and pulls out a bottle of baby powder. The sweet smell of the powder overpowers the urine, which I am beyond thankful for. After he finishes with the powder, he places the bottle back inside of the diaper bag and pulls out a fresh diaper that's covered in blue toy trains. He secures the diaper on his son, who now cries even louder on the cold sink top. When he gets finished, he balls up the used diaper and picks Julio up.

"Do you mind if I put this in there?" He points to a beat-up black trash can that's in the corner of the room. It's completely empty, with not even a trash bag inside of it.

"Sure, knock yourself out," I say. He tosses the heavy, wet diaper into the hollow trash can, where it lands with a loud thud and sends a cloud of dust up into the air.

"Thanks a lot, Miles. He was starting to get fussy with that nasty diaper on," Mr. Rodriguez says as he brushes past me and goes back out into the hallway. I turn off the light in the abandoned restroom, follow after him, and shut the creaky door behind us.

"So, what do you think about this red rain? I've never seen anything like it in my life. And whatever those demonic looking creatures are... I feel like the end times are beginning." His voice fades out and he mumbles something that sounds like Spanish under his breath. A shiver unexpectedly runs up my spine, which almost makes me jump out of my skin.

"I honestly have no idea. I just hope it doesn't spread any more, but something tells me that it will," I think of the video from LA with the lady screaming at the top of her lungs and imagine how terrible it would be if that happened all over the world. "At least we're not in any immediate danger right now since Jaden..." I stop talking when I realize that I almost just revealed what happened downstairs. I gulp.

"Since Jaden hasn't fully turned into one of those things yet," I finish. A thin sheet of sweat breaks out on my forehead and my heart threatens to beat out of my chest. Mr. Rodriguez stares at me for a second too long, which makes me think that he's figured out the truth. Thankfully, Julio cries out again and distracts him before he has time to think of any more questions to ask me.

Mr. Rodriguez reaches inside of a compartment on the diaper bag and pulls out a yellow pacifier. He pops it into Julio's mouth, who happily accepts it, and doesn't cry for the remainder of our walk back to the group.

When we rejoin everyone, it seems like nothing has really changed, except now more people are standing up than sitting down. A few seconds later, Mr. Vega returns from turning off the projectors, with an angry looking Spencer and Amalia in tow behind him. I walk up to Trevor, who stands off to the side by himself, away from Scarlett and Salem.

"Did I miss anything?" I ask him before I realize that he's listening to music on his phone and can't hear me. I tap his shoulder and motion for him to take out the earphones.

"What?" he asks, removing the white earphones one at a time. He doesn't seem irritated to see me anymore. I guess the whole almost dying by deranged psychopath thing canceled his anger toward me.

"Did anything happen while I was gone?" I repeat, a little louder this time.

"Nah. People have started to get restless though. I wish the police would hurry up and get here. I'm worried sick about my parents." He wraps the earphones around his phone and shoves it back into his pocket.

"I'm worried about Mom too. When I talked to her earlier, she said people came in covered with the red rain. I just hope that none of them have started to change yet," I say just as Amalia and Spencer snake their way through the crowd until they're back with us. They walk over to the wall and sit back down, talking to each other as if nothing happened.

"I have good and bad news, everyone," Mr. Vega suddenly exclaims in a sing-songy voice, as if he's addressing a classroom of Kindergarten students. "The good news is that I bravely cracked open one of the exit doors that we have up here and saw that the rain has completely stopped. However, the bad news is that everything, and I mean literally everything, is covered in the rain. The lights have turned on outside and unfortunately, the parking lot looks like it's covered in a lake of blood." Shocked whispers spread throughout the crowd.

"So how are we supposed to get out of here then?" A man asks. I realize that it's Mr. Fisher, my barber, still holding the food that he bought before his movie started. Ella notices him at the same time that I do and takes a few steps backwards to blend in with the crowd, most likely still embarrassed from when she assumed he was my dad.

"Let's just hang tight until the police arrive, which should be any minute now," he pauses to glance down at the gold watch on his wrist, "They mentioned something about bringing protective clothing for everyone, but the connection was a little iffy, so I'm not sure if they heard me give an estimate of the number of people in the building. Hopefully, they come well-prepared," he says and then pauses to dry his forehead with a handkerchief from his pocket.

"How do they plan to deal with that freak of nature downstairs? I will not bring my children out of here until it is completely safe," a young, olive skinned lady says. She holds a baby carrier and a little girl clings to her leg, slightly pulling down her jeans and revealing a pink thong. Two teenaged boys behind her snicker immaturely. One of them pulls out a phone and tries to snap a picture, but the flash goes off and he immediately jerks it away from the woman's butt. The lady turns around furiously when the flash causes her daughter let go of her leg to rub the brightness from her eyes.

"I'm trying to make sure that it'll be safe for my kids and this is what you're focused on? How disrespectful." She pulls her shirt down over the back of her pants as the boy nervously tries to force the phone back into his pocket. She turns back around and makes her daughter stand in front of her.

"Ma'am, I am so sorry about that. When we get downstairs, I'll take down their names and make sure they get banned from coming here for a while," Mr. Vega says to the embarrassed looking lady. Before she can reply, someone knocks on the door right next to where Mr. Vega stands making his announcement. The knocks come in quick succession, a total of four times. The police have finally arrived.

"Ah. That must be the police," Mr. Vega says before he cracks the door open slightly, just enough for him to see out of it. The moment the door opens, a black spike plunges into the room and comes centimeters from Mr. Vega's chest. He tries to slam the door shut, but the creature pushes back, loudly screeching as it tries desperately to get inside.

"Help me! I can't hold it much longer," Mr. Vega screams, using his noodle arms to hold the powerful thing back. The only reason that he's able to keep the creature from coming inside is because the black spikes are too long to fit through the narrow doorway, scraping against the doorframe. Several people toward the front of the group join him in trying to force the door closed and it finally slams with a satisfying thud after about thirty seconds of struggling with it.

A spike is severed when the door closes and falls down to the floor with a wet, sickly splash. Blood seeps from the spot where it was cut off and spreads across the white floor like sauce on a pizza. It looks terrifying, with several black thorns that jut off of it.

When Mr. Vega takes a step back, his tie falls to the floor in tattered pieces, sliced clean through by the sharp spike. The customers closest to the door move away and back down the hallway frantically. The air fills with screams and curses as people process just how close we came to certain death.

"Everyone, quiet! Listen!" Mr. Vega shouts over the panicked crowd.

The door vibrates, still being knocked on in sets of fours. Knock. Knock. Knock. Knock. Pause. The cycle repeats every few seconds and grows progressively louder each time it starts over again.

I feel myself get lightheaded while we wait for the third set of knocks to begin and realize that I'm holding my breath. I quickly exhale and continue to stare at the door, praying that it doesn't come off the hinges.

"Everyone, follow me. We can't stay right here," Mr. Vega says, as he pushes the filing cabinet in front of the door, and then turns around to go down the small flight of stairs that leads to the other projectors. He doesn't urge us to stay calm this time. The crowd surges forward and flows down the stairs after him. The pace slows to a crawl when Ms. Suzanne's group makes it to the top of the staircase, which leaves those of us at the back of the crowd dangerously close to the door of death.

"Hurry up, Golden Girls." The scraggly man who confronted me about keeping secrets earlier yells at the group of five women. The gangly looking woman that he's with lets out an ugly hyena laugh.

"How would you feel if that was your grandmother? Show some respect," I reply to him.

"If that was my grandmother, I would run her right over. She used to beat me with a wooden spoon." When he screams back at me, the knocks on the door grow even louder. Knock. Knock. Knock. Knock. Pause. Knock. Knock. Knock. Knock. Pause.

The people that stand closest to the door push forward, just as the last lady in Ms. Suzanne's group reaches the bottom step. Trevor taps my shoulder.

"How the hell did that thing get up here? And how did it know to knock four times on the door?" he asks.

"I have no idea. Maybe it has super hearing or something," I say

"You don't think Jaden survived those direct headshots, do you?" he whispers to me, even though the only people in earshot are the triplets and Amalia.

"No way. We've both played more than enough video games to know that there is no getting up from that, unless he got some kind of extreme healing power with his transformation. Plus, the one that just tried to get in was wearing a bright green shirt," I say as I think about the sound the razor sharp spikes made when they rubbed up against the wall. The hairs on both of my arms rise up when I picture the piercing yellow eyes dart back and forth across the faces in the crowd, like a butcher examining a pen of cattle waiting to be slaughtered.

We are the very last people to go down the four-step staircase behind the rest of the crowd. "This is the worst day ever. I hope it's safe where Granny Alice is. We should've never left her," Amalia says sadly, once again dropping her usually tough tone of voice.

"Oh, don't start to blame yourself. We had no way of knowing that this would happen," Spencer says as we come to a stop by the projector that runs auditorium four. The group extends all the way up to the exit door that is next to auditorium one. Mr. Vega paces along the wall as he waits for everyone to settle down before he begins to talk again.

"So the way I see it, we have two options. We can either stay up here and hope that the door holds up or we can risk going outside to face whatever might be out there. And it's dark, even with the parking lot lights on," the manager says.

"Think we should make a run for it?" Spencer asks Amalia, who whispers a response into his ear.

"Keep in mind that we don't all have to stick together. Do what you think is best for yourself and those that you're with. Some of you may feel safer at home. This goes for employees too. I won't hold it against you." His eyes land on Ella and Simon first, and then bounce to Trevor and I. We stare back at him and don't respond.

A man in the middle of the crowd speaks up, "I have to be up for work in four hours. I didn't plan to stay here all night," he says with slight hostility in his voice, as if Mr. Vega didn't just say that he's free to leave if he wants to. Unlike this man, the last thing on my mind is work right now, even though I'm at my job.

"Sir, I'll open this door right now and let you walk right out. You can call up here tomorrow if everything is back to normal and I'll have a free guest pass waiting with your name on it. Just keep in mind that it may be incredibly dangerous out there." The man makes his way to the exit door, stops in front of Mr. Vega, and lets out a deep sigh.

"Wow, I wish I was off tomorrow. I can't lose this job," he says out loud, trying to gather himself before he steps outside into whatever horrors the night may hold.

"What do you want to do? Stay or leave?" Trevor asks me. If I ran as fast as I possibly could, I think I would be able to make it to my car without dying. But knowing my luck, I would slip and land face first in a huge puddle of the red rain.

"I really want to leave and go to the hospital to see if Mom is okay. But I know she would kill me if she knew that I left a secure place to look for her," I say.

"I don't really feel secure up here. That door will not last long if that thing doesn't stop beating on it," he says. "What are y'all going to do?" he asks, turning to Spencer and Amalia.

"I think we'll stay here at least for another hour or so. I'm not trying to get caught by one of those things running blindly through the night," Spencer says just as Mr. Vega reaches for the door handle to let the man out. First, he cracks the door open to make sure that it's safe before he lets the man exit. When he sees that there is nothing outside, he widens the sliver until the door is fully open and the man steps out onto the metal staircase with a quick glance over his shoulder.

The temperature has dropped even more since the last time I went outside. Mr. Vega keeps the door open and looks out for the minute or so that it takes the man to reach his vehicle, which allows frigid gusts of wind to come in. It blows so hard that he struggles to keep the door open and his teeth chatter. He slams the door with a thud and turns back to face the shivering crowd.

"Well, that wasn't so bad. Now, is there anyone who wishes to follow him?" he asks with a nervous chuckle and then rubs his hands together to warm them.

CHAPTER 7

After about thirty minutes, the crowd has drastically thinned out. Only Mr. Vega, the elderly people from Ms. Suzanne's group, the triplets and Amalia, Mr. Rodriguez's family, and Trevor and I remain upstairs. After the first man left out, people saw that it might not be as dangerous as we originally thought. Luckily, no one slipped and fell into any of the dark red puddles either. Even Ella finally built up the courage to go home.

Mr. Vega walks up, returning from checking to see if the creature was still lurking around the entrance to the projection booth. He says that the knocking has stopped and that it's eerily quiet on the other side of the door, which he says he didn't dare to open.

"I'm ready to go," Amalia groans.

"Let's just wait one more hour and if nothing happens, we will," Spencer says.

"Fine. I'm hungry and I bet Granny Alice is worried sick," she says, sliding down the wall.

"I don't want to leave right now because if we run into trouble out there, these two won't be able to out run it," he says.

Salem glares at her brother. "You know we're sitting right here, right? We can hear you. How do you know you would be able to out run it? Those things are fast and powerful," she says.

"Hey, I'm just telling the truth. You two aren't ready for the apocalypse or whatever this is."

"You are such an encouraging brother. Admit that you're just using us an excuse and that you're too scared to go out there," Scarlett says.

"Do you three ever give it a break? This constant arguing is really starting to get old," I say, reconsidering my decision to stay here.

"It's like this all the time," Amalia says with a roll of her eyes.

"Are you sure you want to stay here?" Trevor asks, reading my mind.

"Actually, I think I've changed my mind. I'm going to leave," I say to him, jumping to my feet.

"Where are you going?" Amalia asks me.

I hesitate. On one hand, I don't want them to follow me to the hospital, but I also would feel much better out there if I wasn't alone. "To the hospital to find my mother," I say to her. Trevor stands up next to me.

"Your mom is in the hospital?" Spencer asks.

"She's a nurse," I say.

"You didn't think to mention that when I told you about Amalia's grandmother?" he asks, visibly annoyed.

"I didn't think it was important or relevant to the conversation," I fire back, walking toward the door to the leave the building.

"Hold on. Since we're all headed to the same place, I don't think it would be such a terrible idea if we stuck together, just in case we run into any trouble on the way there, and then we can go our separate ways," Spencer says, stands up, and stretches his muscles. The three girls jump to their feet, excited for the chance to finally leave this stale-aired projection booth.

"Fine, but I won't drive slow for you to keep up," I say to him. Trevor walks by my side as we go to tell Mr. Vega that the time has come for us to leave. I nod and smile at the Rodriguez family as I pass by them. Both of the little boys are asleep in their parents' arms.

"We're about to head out, Mr. V," I say when we come to a stop in front of the manager. His large forehead glistens and he's taken off his heavy suit jacket to reveal a sweat-stained mint green shirt.

"All of you are leaving together?" he asks, looking over my shoulder. Spencer and Amalia hold hands, and the two sisters stand closely behind them.

"Yes. My mom worked tonight and they're headed to the hospital too, so we decided it might be safer to follow each other there," I say.

"Do you want to call first before you leave? I'm sure Ms. Suzanne wouldn't mind letting us use her phone again," he says with a concerned look on his face.

"Uh, sure, I guess it wouldn't hurt," I say. He walks to where the elderly lady sits with her group, but returns seconds later empty-handed.

"She says that it died shortly after I used it to call the police, or whoever was actually at the receiving end of that call," he says and lowers his eyes down to the floor. "Are you sure about this?"

"Yes," I lie. "We'll be fine."

"Okay. Be careful. I would offer you some trash bags to put over your clothes, just in case, but we don't have any up here."

"Oh, one more thing. I forgot to clock out," I say with one foot out of the door, placing it on the concrete that leads to the metal staircase that'll then lead us down to the parking lot.

"Me too," Trevor chimes in.

"No problem, I'll fix it later. Please don't die," he says to both of us with a half smile.

"We'll try," I say with a forced laugh.

When I step outside, a strong gust of wind immediately tries to force me back inside the building. I hope this isn't a sign.

I begin my descent down the long staircase, moving at the pace of a snail since I can't use the wet railing to steady my balance. "Guys, I wouldn't touch this railing. It's dripping wet and we probably shouldn't get this stuff on our skin," I say, slightly turning my head to talk over my shoulder, but not enough to be at risk of losing my balance. I wish Trevor would've kept that box of gloves from earlier.

"Really? I was going to lick it clean." Amalia shouts over the howling wind.

I look out into the line of trees behind the building and half expect the creature that Trevor saw earlier to charge out and bound up the stairs to murder us. Luckily, that doesn't happen, and nothing moves in the dark woods.

After what feels like an eternity at the pace we go, we finally reach the bottom of the stairs. "So, where did you park?" I ask Spencer when he steps off of the last stair.

"At the front of the building, toward the edge of the parking lot," he says.

"Me too." I start toward the front of building, with a final glance up at Mr. Vega who watches over us from the top of the stairs. Trevor and I wave up at him, and then he disappears back into the building.

"Are you going to come to the hospital with us or go straight home?" I ask Trevor.

He sighs. "I guess I'll go to the hospital since it's on my way home anyway. Hopefully they have a phone that works there," he says as we round the corner to the front of the building. I look inside and see absolutely no movement, with no sign of the man who shot Jaden. Both spots next to my car are empty and the green SUV is nowhere to be found in the parking lot.

"Let's go," I say, walking ahead of everyone to my car. Trevor's truck sits directly in the row behind me by itself.

"This yours? Nice," Salem says, eyeballing my car.

"Thanks. My grandfather bought it for me."

"I wish our grandparents were that awesome. We're lucky if we even get a phone call on our birthday," Scarlett says, walking around a puddle that is a deep, dark red underneath the parking lot lights. *I wonder why*, I think to myself.

The entire parking lot is covered in puddles similar to the one that Scarlett just went around, some much larger than others. In the center of the lot sits a huge spot that looks like a mini lake. Only a few other vehicles remain in the lot, for the remaining customers that decided to stay in the building with Mr. Vega.

"We'll be right behind you," Spencer says as they walk away from Trevor and I to a black minivan that is by itself a couple of rows behind us. I use the bottom of my shirt to wipe the moisture off of the handle of the driver's door and pull the keys from my pocket to unlock the door.

Before I put the key in the ignition, Trevor slams the door to his truck and the light from his headlights floods the interior of my car. I turn the key, the engine roars to life, and before I shift the car into drive, I crank up the heater to the highest possible setting. I exhale and my breath fills the inside of the car, frosting up the windshield and windows. It's incredibly hard to believe that I couldn't even walk out of the house this morning without immediately breaking into a sweat. I turn on the windshield wipers to clear the sheet of red rain from the glass.

I drive to the parking lot's exit, with Trevor directly behind me, and Spencer joins in closely behind him. Instead of the usual overplayed songs, the only thing that comes out of the radio is deafening static. I flip through the other stations, but none of them work and the white noise seems to grow even louder. Usually, when a station fades out, bits and pieces of the dying song pierce through the loud clutter, but this time the static remains consistent. I turn the volume all the way down as I make a right turn out onto the wet street. I look up into the rearview mirror and watch the flashing blue lights on the theater fade into the night as my car travels farther away from the building.

Briskwood General Hospital is about fifteen minutes away from the theater, but it'll probably take us even less time since it appears that we have the road to ourselves. I know this isn't New York City, the city that never sleeps, but I expected more than just our three vehicles to be on the road. I actually thought the streets would be packed, filled with honking cars and screaming people trying to evacuate the city to escape from whatever is going on.

I pull into the center lane, going slower than I told Spencer I would, but the slick road won't allow me to go much faster without sending the car spinning into a ditch. Most of the houses on both sides of the road are dark inside like any other night. Maybe the families are asleep, unaware of the chaos all around them.

I look at the clock on the radio and see that it's almost 1:00. If Mom is still at work, if the hospital is even still standing, then it's nearly time for her to get off. I press down just a little harder on the gas pedal and send sprays of dark mist flying onto perfectly trimmed lawns. I stop at a red light, wait for it to turn green, and then make a left turn to leave behind the small residential neighborhood and get onto a long, winding highway.

The two sides of the highway couldn't be more different, with an open rice field on one side and a thick forest of trees on the other. The hospital isn't very far from where we are now. It sits right next to a strip mall that's a few miles away from here.

I peel my eyes away from the bare stretch of road for a split second to fiddle with the radio again, hoping that the AM channel will be working since the FM isn't. Once again, static fills the car. I look up just in time to slam on my brakes and avoid smashing into three deer that suddenly run full speed out of the forest.

My car skids off the road, hits a patch of mud, and almost crashes into one of the bulky trees. Either Trevor or Spencer lays on their horn behind me. I turn around and see the two vehicles at a stop on the road, their headlights the only reason that I can make out anything at all on this poorly lit stretch of highway.

My heart pounds and a steady rush of blood throbs in my ears. I throw the car into reverse to get back into position in front of Trevor's truck, thankful that the front of the car isn't deeply embedded into a tree trunk.

Only the tail end of my car is back on the road when I notice that something isn't right. Inside the forest, at least a dozen pairs of blinking yellow eyes stare out at our vehicles. At the edge of the first line of trees lies a fourth deer, a dark brown doe. Under the glow of my headlights, the doe desperately struggles to get up, with one of its front legs bent at an awkward angle underneath it. The terrified animal bleats loudly and uses every ounce of its strength to try and stand up on the broken limb.

Two pairs of the yellow eyes move closer to the edge of the forest, slowly at first as if whatever they belong to wants to scope out the scene, and then picks up the pace the closer they get. Then, a female creature bursts out of the trees, donning a filthy pink dress that is ripped to shreds, with pieces of fabric that drag along the wet ground. The she-beast is maybe seven or eight feet tall, if not even taller. At first, she inches around the doe to further assess the situation and then moves at lightning speed until she stands directly above the animal.

Her skin is a sickly gray color, filled with gashes and cuts where the spikes don't stick out. She's barefoot; the shoes have probably been discarded in a dark corner of the forest after the woman grew to this new, intimidating size. I think back to Jaden's still body on the floor, with only two spikes, still his same size, and figure that the significant height increase must take place at a later stage of the transformation.

The creature goes still, and then lowers her pointed head to sniff the squirming deer. After a few seconds, she stands back up straight and uses one of the spikes on her arms to poke the terrified animal, which causes a spot of red blood to blossom on its back. The creature leans down again, this time with her black tongue extended, and licks the open wound. She jumps up almost faster than my eyes can follow, tilts her head back, and then lets out a blood-chilling, in-human howl so loud that it causes a flock of birds up in the trees to fly off into the night.

Five more of the creatures, three males and two females, emerge from the trees, and go to stand by the side of Pink Dress who appears to be the leader. None of the others are quite as large as Pink Dress, with only one of the males being tall enough to reach her shoulder. One of the smaller females lets out a demonic cackle and grabs the deer's injured leg. Her laughter only intensifies when the animal screams out in pain. The other four creatures circle the deer like a pack of lions, with Pink Dress remaining at the forefront of the group.

I stomp on the gas and my car jumps back into position in front of Trevor, a safe distance away from the disturbing scene. The last thing I see before I peel off down the road is the doe slung over the shoulder of Pink Dress, being carried off to God knows where. I speed, dangerously ignoring the wet road. The only thought in my mind is to get as far away from here as possible.

I glance up into the rearview mirror. Trevor and Spencer are pretty far back, unable to keep up with the engine in my car, so I slow down just a little to allow them to get closer to me. After a few minutes, the trees thin out and open up to reveal the strip mall, which is completely dark and barely has any cars in the parking lot. I stop at a red light directly in front of Abercrombie & Fitch, where an unsmiling model on a billboard glares down at me, as if she's disappointed by the way I lead the group.

The light turns green and I hit a large puddle when I speed off, which sends a sheet of red liquid all over my windshield. I have to turn on the windshield wipers again to send the hellish rain back to the ground, which leaves the glass streaked with pink lines.

Then, a SWAT helicopter appears, flying low with an officer hanging from the side of it screaming a message into a bullhorn. "ATTENTION, CITZENS OF BRISKWOOD. THE HOSPITAL IS BEING CONVERTED INTO A SAFE

HAVEN. THE CITY IS UNDER QUARANTINE. YOU MAY NOT LEAVE." That explains why no one is on the road. The helicopter flies off into the distance, with the officer repeating the message over and over.

The hospital is just over a small hill that is directly in front of me. I stop the car for a brief second and bow my head to say a silent prayer that we're not about to drive into a large-scale version of the scene we just left behind at the edge of the forest. Trevor honks his horn behind me just as I finish. I press the gas and easily clear the small hill.

SWAT and police vehicles surround the hospital, forming a barricade that goes around the entire building. Flashing emergency lights fill the night sky, but it is strangely silent and I don't hear any sirens. Now I see why the neighborhood that we passed on the way here looked so quiet; they're all probably here. The parking lot is fuller than I've ever seen it before and the only open spots are on the very last aisle. I squeeze my car into a tight space, directly under a light, which luckily has two open spots next to it that Trevor and Spencer pull into. I kill the engine and get out, loudly slamming the door behind me.

This large gathering of people makes me nervous, even with the SWAT team here. If a pack of those creatures attacked right now, it would be over for all of us. I just want to find Mom and get the hell away from here, to a more secluded place. Around the huge barricade, Red Cross tents are set up in the grass around the building. People are everywhere, from milling around the tents to standing as close to the hospital as the impenetrable barricade of vehicles will allow.

"That was crazy back there with those deer. I thought those things were gonna go after you next," Trevor says when he gets out of his truck and walks up behind me. Spencer turns off the van and comes to join Trevor and I, with his sisters and Amalia right behind him.

"They were hunting like a pack of wolves. I think the huge one in that ripped up pink dress was the leader," I say.

"Good thing you didn't hit one of those trees. Those things would've swarmed your car and it would've been over," Spencer says.

"Thanks for the optimism," I say with a glare, just as the bone-chilling wind picks up and causes tears to form in my eyes.

Amalia rubs her bare arms. "I left all of my jackets in Louisiana. It's summer, so why is it freezing? Today makes no sense," she says through chattering teeth.

"Global cooling? Caused by the rain?" Trevor says jokingly.

"That isn't a thing. You should try reading books sometimes. It's fun, I'll let you borrow one of mine when all of this is over," Salem says and punches his arm like they're old friends.

We walk toward the massive crowd that gathers around the hospital. It looks like the entire city is here. A man that wears a SWAT uniform stands at the edge of the crowd, so I figure that we should talk to him before we fight our way through the mass of people just to be turned around at the front.

"Excuse me, sir," I say to the straight-faced, expressionless man. He wears a pair of dark sunglasses even though it's pitch black out here.

"We're about to make an announcement in a few minutes. Please join the rest of the crowd," he says authoritatively. I can tell that there will be no way to negotiate with this guy, but I still try to anyway.

"You don't understand. My mom works in the hospital and my phone doesn't work so I can't call her." He removes the sunglasses and stares at me with glassy blue eyes, probably to try and figure out if I'm lying or not.

"Go to one of those white tents. They'll have more information for you there. Tell them that your mom works in the hospital." He points to the closest tent, which is about thirty feet away from here, and then puts the sunglasses back on.

I pick up bits and pieces of conversation as I slowly force my way through the crowd of people, many of whom act like they don't want to move. I pass by a homeless man named Robbie, who I recognize because he always begs for money in public parking lots around town and preaches to anyone who's willing to listen to him. Right now, he stands off to the side by himself, screaming a sermon about how the devil's creatures are about to take over and how we all need to repent before it's too late. People try to ignore him and I notice that a lot of them only steal quick glances in his direction every few seconds.

"You might think I'm crazy, but I'm not! One of those pointed demons got right in my face with those feverish, yellow eyes! I smelled the rotting flesh on its breath!" Robbie yells directly into my ear as I walk by him. A wet, gooey string of spit lands on my cheek, which causes my face to twist up in disgust. Scarlett and Salem both laugh at me when I use the top of my shirt to dry the wet spot on my face.

"Shut up. You're scaring my son." A lady screams behind me. Robbie suddenly stops yelling and when I turn around, two SWAT officers have dragged him away from the crowd.

"They all think he's crazy, but I don't doubt him for a second. Not after what we saw back there with the deer. Except, he definitely didn't come face to face with one of those things or he wouldn't be here to talk about it," Trevor says as we walk into the large tent, which only has a few people inside of it. A short, stubby lady sits alone at a table that has medical supplies laid out on it. She looks bored and unbothered, especially given the current circumstances.

"Hi. One of the SWAT guys told me to come in here for more information about what's going on in the hospital," I say.

"Do you have a relative inside of the building right now?" she asks dryly before she breaks into a deep smoker's cough. I allow her to stop and take a few gulps of water before I answer.

"Yes. My mom, Cheryl Walton, works in the hospital as a nurse," I say, not trying to hide any of the concern in my voice so I can get as much information as possible. She stands up and grabs a folded piece of paper from the table. She's even shorter than she looked when she was seated; I tower over her by at least a foot.

"Follow me. And only you." She glares behind me when Trevor and the rest of the group try to follow us.

"Wait. My grandmother is inside of the hospital too," Amalia says, walking away from Spencer's side to stand by me.

"Well, you can come, but the rest of you stay put," the lady says. We go out of a flap at the back of the tent and leave the others behind. It's eerily quiet back here, with no one else in sight.

"Was that really necessary? Trevor is my be— "

"Yes," she interrupts without turning around to face me. She walks until we're far enough from the tent so that no one can hear us.

"I'm Sally Benoit with the Red Cross. People came into the hospital soaked with red rain and a few of them turned into threaders. The inside of the building looks like a war zone. It's an absolute disaster." She starts her speech and then breaks into another fit of coughing.

"Threaders? What does that mean?" I ask, too scared to immediately ask if there were any casualties. The fact that we're so far out of earshot from the others already answers that question.

"That's what the news calls them. Well, that's what they were calling them before the TV's and phones stopped working a few hours ago. They call them threaders because of the way they create more of their own, expand their numbers. When they select a victim, they slice the person up, inject them with this green slime that oozes from their skin, and then sews them back together with this silk that comes out of those black spikes. It's like their way of reproducing. Gruesome stuff."

"Did anyone inside of the hospital get hurt?" I finally ask, my voice cracking.

"Oh God, yes. I have a list of all of the confirmed fatalities right here. But I'm not sure if anyone has turned into a threader. It's an unorganized situation right now, but I suppose it's possible." She unfolds the sheet of paper that's in her hand. The planet shifts under my feet and my heartbeat quickens. I force myself to take a deep breath as she reads the list.

"What did you say your mom's name is? Wallis? Wilson?" she asks.

"Walton. Cheryl Walton," I repeat. She reads the papers carefully, for what is easily the longest five seconds of my life.

"No Walton on here," she says and I breathe a sigh of relief.

"Don't get too excited yet. The threaders are still in the building, so this list could already be outdated, plus we still don't know if anyone has changed since there really isn't any way to safely identify them. The SWAT team is inside right now trying to contain the situation before they come out to inform everyone who doesn't have family inside about what happened. About thirty SWAT officers are inside of the building. Half of them had to hold those monsters at bay while the rest went around to identify the victims. A few of them cried when they came to deliver this list to me. This was the first time I had ever seen that. They're usually tough as nails," she says to me before she turns her full attention to Amalia, who nervously chews on a red braid of hair. "What is your grandmother's name, darling?"

"Alice Stephenson. She's a cancer patient," Amalia says.

Sally's unsmiling face crinkles up even more when the words are out of Amalia's mouth. She clears her throat before she speaks. "I'm sorry to tell you this, but the oncology unit is right next to the emergency room where the patients turned. It has been completely destroyed and unfortunately, none of the patients that were receiving treatment survived. I'm deeply sorry for your loss," she says in a much more professional and rehearsed voice than when she spoke to me, as if she's used to having to deliver this kind of news.

"Wh-what?" Amalia stammers. "This has to be some kind of mistake. She can't be dead. Are you positive that there were no survivors?" she continues, almost hysterical.

"I'm afraid not. The SWAT team did a complete walk-through and—" Before she can finish, Amalia bolts back into the tent and leaves us standing alone in the cold night.

I turn my head away from Sally to hide the tears that form in my eyes. That could've easily been my mom. It could still be my mom.

"She your girlfriend?" Sally asks me as I rub the tears away, pretending that a stray eyelash caused them to water up.

"No. A customer at my job that I just met tonight," I quickly say.

"Oh. Well before she stormed off, I was going to tell her that we have grief counselors on site," she says.

"What is being done to help the remaining survivors inside?" I ask.

"There is a team inside trying to... secure the area. But it's tricky. These things are hard to kill and they also seem to have retained all, if not more, of their intelligence from when they were still human. We've already lost several high-ranking officers to these monsters. Good men and women. The only thing that seems to get the job done is a bullet to the back of the head. Less of those disgusting spikes there." I think of the man that aimed the gun directly at the back of Jaden's skull and then ended his life with the pull of a trigger.

"Did they try to put them into quarantine first?" I ask, my stomach sinking.

"If you saw the pictures that the officers took, you would know that setting up a quarantine is not possible. There is no negotiating with these things and tranquilizers don't seem to work either." She pauses to shake her head, maybe to rid her mind of disturbing mental images. "They might still be intelligent, but there are no human feelings left inside of them."

"So, why is the SWAT team allowing a huge group of nervous people to gather right outside of the building?" I ask her.

"They don't have that many left to neutralize. It's just as dangerous out here right now as it is in there. Once all of the threats inside have been eliminated, we're going to bring everyone inside to explain what happened. It'll be safer inside since we have the barricade around the hospital. I just hope they hurry up before anyone else gets hurt. It feels like the whole damn city is here."

"This is scary. I agree that they need to hurry up because I saw some of those... threaders in action on the way here and it was not a pretty sight." I say, remembering the doomed doe.

"Everyone is doing the best that they can. None of us have ever dealt with a situation like this before," she says as we turn around and go back into the tent.

Amalia sobs into Spencer's chest. He softly strokes her hair with one hand and rubs the other up and down her back. I feel terrible for her. Her cries, which grow louder by the second, make it painfully obvious that she was close to her grandmother. Trevor looks pretty upset too, awkwardly standing off to the side by himself. Scarlett and Salem stand near the entrance to the tent, quietly talking to each other.

Sally walks up and places a hand on Amalia's shoulder. "We have grief counselors available if you want to talk to someone, honey. They're set up in another tent a little ways from here."

"I don't feel like talking to anyone," Amalia says, lifting her head from Spencer's drenched shirt. Sally pulls a small pack of tissues from her pocket and gives them to her. She wipes some of the tears and snot from her face, only to undo the clean up seconds later when she collapses into another round of sobs. I decide to let Spencer do all of the comforting, at least for right now anyway, and pull Trevor to the side to fill him in on the new information I gained from Sally. When I finish, his mouth is wide open in shock.

"So they're just murdering people? What did you call them? Throttlers?" he asks a little too loudly, which causes me to receive a stern glare from Sally.

"Threaders. Keep your voice down. They want to keep this quiet right now. I'm pretty sure Sally only told me because my mom is in immediate danger," I whisper.

"This is crazy. Did she say if people are just being killed or turned into threaders? That's such a strange word. How do they come up with these things?" he asks, more to himself than to me.

"She didn't know. She kept using words like 'eliminate' and 'neutralize,' but they're not sure if any of the employees or patients that were already admitted to the hospital have been changed," I mumble. My mind is not on this conversation at all because of how worried I am about Mom, probably trapped somewhere and scared for her life.

"Are you holding up okay? I'm sure your mom will be fine," Trevor asks when he notices my lack of enthusiasm.

"Thanks, but please don't get my hopes up. You saw what happened to that deer back there and if people are trapped inside of a building with those things..." I let the dark thought hang in the air for a few seconds. "I just hope she found somewhere safe to hide until the building is clear," I finish.

After that, we don't talk for a few minutes. The only sounds come from Amalia's soft cries and quiet conversations between other people in the tent. Sally is back at the table she was at when we first walked in.

Without thinking, I take a seat on the damp grass. When I look at my hands, they are covered in bright red liquid.

I spring to my feet. Sally sees me suddenly jump up and comes over to me as I quickly rub my hands on my pants to get the red rain off.

"Don't worry. They think the rain has to fall directly from the sky in order for it to change you. It loses its potency once it touches the ground. Sorry, I forgot to mention that earlier," she says and squirts a glob of hand sanitizer onto my outstretched hands. The nonstop stress from today will probably age me a few years in a matter of hours.

"Great. I'm not the best at this apocalypse stuff," I say to her.

I'm talking to Trevor about all of the crazy events of today when a SWAT officer bursts into the tent. The officer walks quickly, almost a jog, until he stops in front of the table that Sally sits at. He bends his tall, skinny body down to where he can whisper something into her ear. When she nods in agreement, he turns around and briskly walks out. I leave Trevor's side and go up to the lady, who now stands up, to see if I can pry some more information out of her.

"More bad news?" I ask.

"Actually, no. They've given the all clear to let these anxious people into the building. All of the threats have been eliminated," she talks extremely fast, stumbling over some of her words. She turns away from me to face the others in the tent before I can ask if they've found any survivors.

"Attention, everyone," she shouts to the small number of people in the tent. Everyone stops what they're doing to look at her. A blonde lady who stands off to the side by herself, crying, lifts her head to reveal sad blue eyes and a mascara streaked face. She's not alone, with tears streaming down the faces of almost everyone in the tent. Amalia rests her head on Spencer's shoulder, no longer crying, but she looks like her soul has been drained from her body.

"First, let me start by extending my deepest condolences to those who have lost a loved one in tonight's tragic events. As you all know, the SWAT team has worked inside to transform the hospital into a safe haven for anyone who wants to stay. I have just been informed that they are now finished and are about to move people in. If you would like to go inside, please rejoin the large group of people directly outside of this tent," Sally says.

"So we're supposed to go into the place where all of those people were murdered? I bet they thought they would be safe in there too. This is so wrong. This is all so wrong," the pretty blonde lady says in a strained, sour voice. She dabs at the lines of mascara on her cheeks with a tissue.

"Look, I didn't say that you have to go inside. Personally, I just think being inside of a building that's surrounded by armored SWAT vehicles is safer than staying in this thin tent where we are completely exposed. This young man right here saw a group of those things on his way here, just a few miles away," Sally replies, motioning to me. My face flushes red when everyone in the tent turns their attention away from her to me.

"Is this true?" the blonde lady asks me.

"Uh, yeah. We saw a group of them surround a deer and carry it off into the forest. They looked like they were having the time of their lives. It was pretty disturbing," I say. Several people's mouths fall open in surprise.

"Well, if we don't want to end up carried off into the woods, I suggest we get moving." Sally puts her hand on the flap of the tent to open it. Through the crack, the night sky is quiet and filled with bright stars, with no sign of the ominous storm clouds that changed people's lives forever. The crowd outside moves slowly forward toward the hospital.

"The grief counselors will be available inside if anyone wants to talk to one," Sally says over her shoulder before another round of coughs consumes her.

"Miles, what part of the hospital does your mom work in?" Amalia has broken away from Spencer's side and now stands next to me as we shuffle out of the tent.

"I think she sticks around the emergency room mostly," I say as I picture Mom standing over a hospital bed with chaos erupting around her.

"I just can't believe this is happening. The doctors said that the treatments were destroying the cancer at a fast rate. And now she's gone," she sobs again and then disappears ahead of us into the slow moving crowd.

"Amalia, wait," Spencer says and tries to follow after her, but Salem grabs his arms and pulls him back.

"Can you give me the keys to the van? I want to grab my purse before we go into the hospital," she says. He reaches into his pocket and pulls out a ring of silver keys, which he hands to his sister without looking at her. She isn't able to get a good grip on them, so they fall to the ground. When she picks up the keys, which were once shiny, they are bathed in dark red liquid.

"Gross. I hope they're right about this stuff being harmless once it reaches the ground. I'll be right back," she says as she rubs her hands on her black T-shirt and then walks away from us. Trevor, Scarlett, and I stand at the edge of the crowd and Spencer is a little farther up, with just the top of Amalia's head visible next to him among the sea of people.

"Think we should wait for her?" I ask.

"Well, duh. I won't leave her like my brother did," Scarlett says bitterly with a roll of her eyes. I look out into the packed parking lot and see a small light on inside of the van. The passenger side door is open for a few seconds before it closes behind Salem.

Almost as soon as the door closes, a single piercing screech rips out of the darkness behind the parking lot, then another, and then more and more until a demon choir fills the air. Before any of us can grasp onto what is happening, it's too late. Salem moves around inside of the van, but I can't tell if she has realized what is going on all around her. Threaders slink into the parking lot from the direction that we drove in from, bounding over cars and weaving in and out of them. Bright sparks flash every time a spike from one of the fast moving creatures connects with the metal of a car.

After about thirty seconds, threaders stand by every vehicle in the parking lot that I can see, their yellow eyes staring intently at the people who move toward the hospital. There have to be at least fifty or sixty of them, with at least one standing at attention by every car. Two smaller ones are by a white truck. They roll around on the ground, playing with each other like children at a park. Then, from behind a red SUV toward the very front of the parking lot, the hulking Pink Dress appears.

When she sees everyone looking in her direction, she turns around to face her minions and lets out another earth trembling roar. At the sound of the roar, the two smaller threaders that play on the ground jump to their feet and the other motionless creatures spring into action as if they're puppets on a string. The crowd that was steadily moving into the hospital now turns into a stampede, with everyone trying desperately to get into the building. Instinctively, I take two steps backwards to follow them, but then stop when I remember that Salem is still in the van. Spencer and Amalia break free from the crowd and rejoin us to look out into the parking lot.

Scarlett tries to go after her sister, but I gently lay a hand on her shoulder to hold her back. "Wait. You can't go out there," I whisper into her ear. I look at Spencer's van and see that the light inside of it is off now. Salem is probably hunkered down inside, realizing that she is no longer safe. "Look. The light in the van is off now. She'll be fine," I say to put her at ease.

When the roar from Pink Dress stops, another sound starts. The threaders rub the spikes on their arms together and create a noise that is worse than nails on a chalkboard. After a few seconds, bright sparks of light flicker through the dark until most of them gradually remain lit. When I look more closely, it becomes evident that the lights are actually flames that lick up and down the black spikes, spreading by the second. The large group of creatures with their flaming spikes reminds me of an angry mob, except they have pitchforks and torches that are combined into one.

"SALEM!" Scarlett screams at the top of her lungs, removing my hand from her shoulder. Spencer jumps forward and wraps his arms around her so that she doesn't run to her certain death.

"Miles…" Trevor starts to say, but another deafening roar drowns the words out. Every moving figure in the parking lot comes to an abrupt halt. For about ten seconds, several dozen sets of piercing yellow eyes stare at the remaining people who wait outside of the hospital to watch the scene unfold. Scarlett sobs in her brother's arms, who also appears to be on the verge of tears himself.

The only movement in the parking lot comes from the bright orange flames that travel up and down the arm spikes of the creatures. Suddenly, Pink Dress spins her huge body around so that her back faces us. With one flaming arm extended, she connects a spike to the SUV and travels alongside the vehicle, which creates a sound that sends chills racing up my spine. I can only imagine the size of the scratch on the body of the SUV and the fact that the spike is on fire probably doesn't help at all either. The screeching goes on until she reaches the back of the vehicle and comes to a stop.

She removes the spike from the side of the SUV and lets it hang limply by her side. For a moment, I think that she's about to walk away. Then, she uses her super strength to plunge the flaming spike directly into the gas tank of the vehicle. The SUV explodes, erupts into a ball of flames, and then flies backwards a few feet. The flames engulf Pink Dress and I'm sure that she has just committed suicide in front of all of us.

When the huge ball of fire recedes back into the SUV after the initial blast, I'm able to make out a hulking gray mass of flesh lying on the ground several feet away. Pieces of flaming pink fabric hang from the spikes, like grotesque candles on a birthday cake. Almost as soon as I'm able to make out her form, she moves. She jumps to her feet and pivots around to face the hospital.

The front of the dress is almost completely gone, revealing much more of her than I ever wanted to see. She tilts her head back like a wolf howling at the moon and lets out a deep, throaty laugh that definitely does not make the chills that are all over my body go away. When she finishes laughing, she does something that I didn't think was possible anymore: she speaks.

"Do it." The two words come out loud enough for every creature in the parking lot to hear her, but they're almost unintelligible, as if this is her first time attempting to speak since the drastic transformation.

All around her, the others begin to recreate exactly what she just did to the SUV. I cup my hands and slam them over my ears when the sound from dozens of spikes scraping against the metal of the cars is almost too much for me to bear. After about thirty seconds, explosions instantly replace the scraping sound when they thrust their spikes into the gas tanks of the vehicles.

"OH MY GOD! SALEM!" I read Spencer's lips since I can't hear a single thing over the tremendous booms that happen every other second.

I turn away from Spencer just in time to see a male threader leap on top of a car in the second row and then slide down the back of it. He reappears seconds later, next to the gas tank of course, and then blows it up. The doors of the small car fly off it, shooting through the air at a fast pace. One of the doors strikes a female threader in the back of the head and tears off several spikes in the process. She falls to the ground and I watch her closely for a few seconds, but she doesn't stand back up.

Spencer, Amalia, and Scarlett have stopped trying to hold in their tears. They're huddled up in a ball on the ground, holding each other as they cry. Trevor stands directly next to me, speechlessly staring out at the carnage. I glance over my shoulder and see that we are the only people who are crazy enough to still be outside. The few remaining people that were out here with us must have gone in once all of the explosions started. A man bangs on the glass inside of the hospital. It looks like he wants us to come in, but I turn back around and ignore him.

The parking lot is an inferno. Flames and smoke cover every vehicle that I can see, rendering them useless and leaving everyone stranded inside of the hospital. I can't tell for sure, but I don't think my car has been touched yet.

The moment my eyes settle on Spencer's van, it explodes. Trevor and I are the only ones who see the explosion since the others are on the ground. I can't tell if Salem was somehow able to make a grand escape, but I have a terrible feeling that she didn't.

"Salem. Salem. Salem. I gave her the keys. I should've walked out there with her," Spencer says in between sobs. Amalia places a hand on his shoulder, but he brushes it off, much to my surprise.

As quickly as all of the explosions start, they stop. A cloud of smoke covers the entire parking lot, as if a supervolcano has just erupted. Flaming threaders are everywhere, standing as if the fire doesn't bother them at all. It appears that they've only suffered one casualty, the female one that was struck in the back of the head with the car door. She hasn't moved an inch from the spot where she fell. Pink Dress lets out one final roar, which must be a command for all of them to leave now that the job is done. All of the threaders run back in the direction that they came from, with many of them still on fire. The parking lot is still once again, but now pieces of metal and burned out vehicles litter the ground.

When I look out into the parking lot, I can confirm that my car is the only one that has been left untouched. The bright red paint on my car sticks out drastically from the burned out black shells of every other vehicle around it, especially since it sits directly underneath a light. Spencer jumps up from the ground and sprints toward what is left of his van.

"I can't see her like that if she got blown up. I'm staying here," Scarlett says, removing her glasses to wipe away some of the tears from her face.

"I'll stay with you," Amalia says, gently rubbing her back.

"Come on," I say to Trevor. We run behind Spencer.

The overturned, burned out vehicles and debris that cover every inch of the concrete parking lot makes it difficult to run in a straight line. It's almost impossible to tell where one row ends and another begins. Trevor and I weave our way through the destroyed vehicles, with Spencer about two or three rows in front of us.

"Spencer, wait up!" If he hears me above the howling wind, he acts like he doesn't and keeps moving. Trevor or I should look into the van first. He might lose it if he sees his sister like that, no matter how badly he treats her.

We're about halfway to the back row when I realize something; there are guns everywhere, mixed in with the bent metal and other debris. This is Texas; people here are extremely passionate about their guns and take them everywhere. I've counted at least ten of them since we started our chase after Spencer.

When we finally reach Spencer, I nearly crash into him when I run from behind a car and trip over a child's half melted booster seat. "Whoa!" I scream as I go down. Thankfully, I land with a thud on one of the few spots on the concrete that isn't littered with scrap metal. I stand up, brush the dirt from my pants, and then walk the few steps that separate me from Spencer. He stares into the remains of his smoking van and doesn't even turn around when I fall.

"There's no body. Maybe she got away," he says in a quiet voice, turning to look at me. There are tears in his eyes. I cough when the wind suddenly changes and blows a cloud of smoke directly into my lungs.

Trevor walks up behind us and goes around to the opposite side of the van to get a better look inside of it. "Guys, come here. You might wanna see this," he says in a slightly panicked voice. Spencer and I go around the back of the van to join him.

He doesn't look inside of the destroyed van anymore, but his attention is now focused on my perfectly intact car. He stands at the front of the car and traces his finger along the hood.

"What are you doing?" I ask when I walk up beside him.

I look down at the hood and gasp.

CHAPTER 8

Engraved onto the car are the words: *Miles. Come with Amalia. Or Salem dies. You will not be harmed.* An arrow that points backwards, in the direction that the threaders ran off in, is scratched into the red paint of the car directly next to the words. There is also a spike speared through the top of the car with a piece of black fabric that hangs from it. I step away from the hood, pull the fabric from the spike to examine it, and see that it's a piece of cloth with a list of tour dates on it. I recognize it from the back of Salem's Lady Gaga T-shirt. I hand it to Spencer, who balls it up in his hand.

"What are we gonna do?" Trevor asks. "You and Amalia can't go out there alone," he continues with a look of concern on his face. I understand why he's so upset, but I can't just let her die. I decide that I have to go after her.

"I have to try," I say slowly, looking directly at Spencer, who hasn't said a word since we read the message on the front of the car. "Unless her brother wants to go in my place. You could take my work shirt and stick to the shadows. They would never know the difference. What do you say?" I pull the car keys from my pocket and dangle them in front of his face. He hesitates for a second before he speaks.

"Look. I would, but it specifically says you and Amalia have to go. They might kill her instantly if I slip up and they see that it's not you," he says, with a twinge of jealousy in his voice. He must wonder why Amalia and I were specifically requested to go after Salem. I realize just how creepy it is that those things know our names. The fact that they look like monsters, but can write and speak deeply disturbs me.

"How do they know our names? What's going on?" Trevor asks, pulling the thoughts directly from my head. I drop my arm and put the keys back into my pocket.

"No idea. Nothing makes any sense right now. How will we even know where to go? An arrow pointing backwards won't get us very far." I say.

Out of nowhere, Trevor screams in pain.

"What's wrong?" Spencer asks.

"Something just burned my leg!" he screams and claws at his pocket. He pulls out the golden pocket watch that he found earlier in the auditorium that we cleaned. "What the... I thought I gave this to Mr. Vega when I went to tell him about the dead birds," he says, dangling the watch by its chain. The small, circular device glows a fiery orange color, flashing every few seconds.

"Why is it glowing like that?" I ask.

"I don't know, but I can't touch it. I'm sure that I have a third degree burn on my leg now," he says, grimacing as he rubs the spot on his pants where the watch was. A few seconds later, the watch stops glowing and returns to its regular golden color.

"Well, go ahead and open it. We don't have all night," I say when he's hesitant to remove his hand from the chain and open the watch.

"No way. If the outside of this thing hurt that much, then I don't want to know what's inside of it. But go ahead, knock yourself out," he says and tosses it to me. It almost slips out of my hands, but I catch it by the chain. When I touch the actual watch, I half expect it to burn the skin off of my fingers, but it's not even slightly warm. In fact, it feels almost as cold as it is outside right now.

On the front of the watch is a sinister gray and black skull. On the back, there are two letters engraved, H and P. When I open it up, I expect to see a regular watch face with ticking hands that remind me of how late that it is right now. I'm surprised that it actually has a digital screen.

The screen is blank except for a small ticking line, which reminds me of a document that waits to be typed on. Right on cue, a message appears on the screen. There is a lag between each word that pops up, as if there is someone on the other end typing out the message. The message is short and straight to the point, basically an elaboration of the one on the hood of my car: *Miles. Come to the theater with Amalia. Or everyone, including Salem, dies.* When I read the message, it fades off of the screen as if it never existed.

"What does it say?" Trevor and Spencer ask at the exact same time, but I dismiss them with the wave of a hand. Spencer steps forward to look at the screen, but I back away from him.

A few seconds later, a picture fills the entire screen. The picture was taken inside of one of the auditoriums at my job. The cleaning lights have been turned on so that it is perfectly clear what is going on. The remaining customers that were inside of the building when I left all sit in the seats of the auditorium.

I use two of my fingers to zoom in on the small picture to see if I can make out any other details. It looks like everyone has been tied down with rope, even the two small children from the Rodriguez family. The picture fades from the screen before I can get a clear look, but I don't see Salem among any of the terrified faces. She's probably still being dragged through the night by the pack of threaders.

One final message pops up on the screen: *They all die if you're not here in one hour. Come with Amalia ONLY.* I wait a few seconds after the screen goes black to make sure that no more words pop up, but none do. I wrap the chain around the watch and jam it into my pocket.

"You don't wanna do that. Trust me," Trevor says, pointing at my leg.

"You're probably right," I say and pull the watch from my pocket. I open my car and drop it into the cup holder.

"Now tell us what was inside of the watch," Spencer says, growing impatient.

"It's not a regular pocket watch, it has a screen like a text message box. I think they're going to bring Salem to the theater. For some reason, only Amalia and I can go after her. If I can convince Amalia, we'll go, but I have to check and see if my mom is okay first. It says that we have an hour, well even less time than that now, until they kill all of the customers that we left behind in the building. And Salem," I say, turning away from them to head back toward the hospital.

"Do you know who sent the message?" Spencer asks, running closely behind me. I nearly trip over a shotgun that lies on the ground near a blown up truck. On my way back, I need to quickly search the parking lot to pick up a few weapons just in case I need them later.

"No. Now stop asking questions so I can go and get your sister," I shout back over my shoulder.

I'm almost completely out of breath when I reach the barricade of vehicles that surrounds the hospital. There is one vehicle missing from the barricade, a black van that is backed out of the line to allow people into the building. A SWAT officer near the front of the building walks up to talk to us when we approach.

"You three barely made it. I came out here to move the van to seal the barricade," she says in a rough, gravelly voice. She wears a black cap, but I can picture her hair wrapped into a severe bun underneath it.

"I'm actually not staying. I just have to see a couple of people that are inside of the building," I say to her.

"Better make it quick. I'm about to seal us in tight. I'll give you ten minutes." I don't see why Amalia (if I can even convince her to go) and I wouldn't just be able to climb right over one of the vehicles and jump down. The threaders would probably charge right through this barricade, destroying the armored vehicles like they did the rest of the parking lot. I don't point this out to the SWAT officer since it would start an argument and I have no time to waste.

"Um, okay, sure. I'll hurry," I say to her instead, suppressing how I really feel. With a nod, she unlocks the van and climbs inside. Spencer and Trevor follow behind me as I step up to the automatic glass doors to enter the hospital.

The inside of the hospital is even colder than it is outside, even with the large mass of people that congregate near the reception area. I scan the crowd, looking specifically for Mom, but my eyes land on Amalia and Scarlett first. They sit in a small lobby directly next to the reception desk, away from most of the crowd. Next to them is a popcorn machine with pre-made bags inside of it. When I walk up to them, the familiar, unwelcome buttery smell enters my nose and drags Jaden's unfortunate fate back into my mind.

Scarlett sobs softly on Amalia's shoulder. When we go up to them, they leap to their feet. "Is she dead?" Scarlett asks.

"Did you find her?" Amalia asks at the exact same time.

"Hold on. Spencer will explain everything. I have to go and find Mom," I say. Spencer glares at me, as if he's angry that he's about to become the bearer of bad news. I have to bite my tongue to stop myself from screaming at him that I'm about to risk my life for his sister and all he has to do is talk about it. As I turn away from them to join the large crowd that surrounds the circulation desk, he begins with the message that we found engraved on the hood of my car.

I have to hurry. Ten minutes have already passed since the final message faded from the screen of the watch. I walk up to the edge of the crowd and have to stand on my tiptoes to find the desk in the middle of the bodies.

There are three nurses seated at the wooden desk. Unfortunately, none of them are Mom. The four computers that sit on the desk are usually lit up and filled with all kinds of medical stuff, but now the screens are as black as the night sky.

I recognize one of the nurses, Vanessa Blakely. Her and Mom got hired around the same time and instantly became friends. She flips through a stack of papers while she talks to several angry looking people at once. I figure that if anyone knows where Mom is, it's Ms. Vanessa. I should talk to her before I waste time searching this whole hospital. I force my way up to the desk until I stand in front of the young, black haired nurse who doesn't notice me at first because she's distracted by the paperwork. I clear my throat loudly.

"Excuse me, Ms. Vanessa. Have you seen my mom anywhere?" I ask. When she hears my voice, she immediately stops looking at the paperwork and jumps to her feet.

"Miles! Your mom is worried sick about you. She called you back after she talked to you the first time, but all of our electronics stopped working," she says, pointing to the dead computers on the desktop. A wave of relief washes over me that is so strong that it almost causes me to faint. I have to place my hand on top of the desk to steady myself.

"Oh, thank God. I've been worried sick about her too. Do you know where she is right now? I have to leave, but I want to see her before I go,"

"Got a hot date to ring in the apocalypse with?" she asks with a wink. I can't think of a single time that I've talked to her when she didn't have an ear-to-ear grin plastered across her face, even in stressful situations like this one.

"No. It's… complicated," I say.

"She just went in there to grab some more papers from the back," She points to a secure looking metal door that is right behind the desk. "She should be back in five minutes or so."

"Okay. I really have to get going. Do you think I could run back there and talk to her really quick?" I ask. An elderly lady that has been glaring at me ever since I forced my way up to the front of the crowd lets out a loud groan. I don't feel great about cutting in front of these worried people, but if I don't hurry, then even more lives will be lost tonight.

"I'm sorry," I say to the old lady, "It's an emergency,"

"We all have an emergency. That's why we're in the lobby of a hospital right now," she says sourly.

"Yeah, buddy. That isn't cool," a balding, middle-aged man says. The old lady gives him a smile, happy to have someone to help back her up.

"I'm sorry. I really am. I wouldn't have cut in front of everyone if it wasn't extremely important," I say to them before I turn back to Ms. Vanessa.

"Authorized personnel only. Sorry," she says, pointing to a large red sign that has the words plastered onto it in bold, white ink.

"Okay. I'm gonna go back over there to the lobby area to talk to those people. If I leave before she comes back, can you tell her that I stopped by?"

"Sure, Miles. Are you sure that you want to go out there though? It's safer in here," she says with so much confidence that I almost forget that so many people were murdered in here less than an hour ago. Up the hall, the emergency room where most of the attack took place is barely visible through the lines of yellow caution tape that the SWAT team must have put up to obscure the view of the destruction. The part of the hospital that we're in looks completely normal, as if the threaders went out of their way to leave it untouched.

"I don't really have a choice. Thanks, Ms. Vanessa." She gives me another smile, but for the first time ever, her happy eyes lose their twinkle. I make my way out of the crowd and go back over to the lobby.

Of course, Amalia and Spencer are engaged in a heated discussion.

"I understand that. What I don't get is why whoever sent that asked specifically for us two," Amalia says as she nervously runs her fingers through her hair and lets out a sigh.

"I'm not sure. But you saw for yourself that those things mean business," Spencer replies to her. Scarlett sits unmoving in the same spot where she listens intently to their conversation. Trevor springs from his seat next to Scarlett when I come up to them.

"Did you find her anywhere?" he asks.

"She's okay. I talked to one of the nurses and she told me that Mom has tried to call me, but couldn't when the phones stopped working. I didn't get to see her though because she's in the back where only employees are allowed." I glance down at my wrist instinctively to look at my watch that isn't there. Even though I don't know exactly what time it is, Amalia and I need to go soon if we plan to save the endangered customers.

"Really? They couldn't make an exception for you?"

"I didn't want to push my luck. I already pissed off a few people off when I forced my way to the front of the group. Didn't want to attract any unwanted attention, especially from those SWAT officers," I say, glancing over my shoulder. Five stoic officers stand toward the exit to the parking lot out front, staring silently at the crowd around the desk. I turn my attention to Spencer and Amalia.

"Guys, not to butt in, but if we're gonna do this, then it has to be now," I say.

"Who said that I'm going anywhere with you?" Amalia asks.

"Now is not the time for this. You can't have an attitude like this when you go out there," Spencer says, which confirms that they've already come to a decision and that Amalia's stubbornness is a defensive mechanism to hide her fear.

"Come on. Lives are at stake. We have to go. Now," I repeat and then turn away from them so that she doesn't have time to start another argument.

"Hold on," Trevor says behind me. I spin around and am met with a bear hug from my best friend, which catches me off guard. "Be careful out there," he says and I notice that tears are in his eyes. I shove him off of me.

"Stop that. I'll be fine. They obviously want me alive, at least for a little while. For some reason, this seems personal to me."

Honestly, for the past few years, things haven't gone that great for me. I don't want to die, but if Amalia and I run into trouble out there, I won't hesitate to save her over myself. If I have to go, I want to go out a hero.

"Do you have a plan or something for when you get there?" Trevor asks as Amalia walks up beside me.

"Nope, haven't really thought that far ahead yet. We can do a little brainstorming in the car. You ready to go?" I ask Amalia.

"I've never been so unprepared for anything in my life, but I guess so. Salem owes us one if we make it out of this alive," she says as she pries off the arm that Spencer has draped around her. She plants a kiss on his lips and then gives Scarlett a half hug.

"Thank you for going after my sister. I don't know what I'll do if something happens to her," Scarlett says to Amalia and I.

I wasn't lucky enough to have any siblings of my own, so I can only imagine how hard this must be for her, especially since they look nearly identical to each other.

"At least it gives me something to think about besides my grandmother," Amalia says softly.

"Why are you doing this, Miles? You don't even know us," Spencer asks with a raised eyebrow.

"Because if I don't, innocent people will die and I could never live with that on my conscience if I knew that I could've at least tried to stop it from happening."

"Take care of her. Please. And try to try bring my sister back in one piece," he says to me, but doesn't take his eyes off of Amalia. With a final look at Trevor, I turn away from them and walk away with Amalia by my side.

"Ms. Vanessa." I shout from behind the wall of people that wait to be helped at the desk. Luckily, I'm tall enough to see over mostly everyone so she spots me immediately when I call out to her. "I'm about to head out." As soon as she opens her mouth to respond, the door behind her cracks open and Mom steps out. When she appears, I realize that I haven't thought of a way to explain to her what I'm about to do. I might as well give her the full truth.

"Mom!" I yell. I leave Amalia's side and Mom leaves from behind the desk to meet me halfway.

"Miles, I'm so relieved that you're okay. I was so scared when the phones went down. I was just about to leave out and come look for you," she says as she embraces me in a tight hug.

"I'm glad I got to you first. It's not really that safe out there," I say, which won't help at all when I explain to her why I have to go back out. "Mom, there's something I have to tell you." She removes her arms from around me and the smile instantly disappears from her face.

"What is it?" She asks. I tell her what I have to do and by the time I finish, tears trickle down her face.

"No. I can't let you go back out there. Not alone with some girl you just met tonight," she whispers.

"I have to, Mom. They were very specific," I say. The tears flow freely from her eyes now.

"Who are they? Do you even know what you're about to walk into?" she asks. The messages on the watch didn't have a signature, so I just assumed that they came from the threaders, that the savage beasts are smarter than they appear to be. My mind has only been set on saving those people and I have no idea what to expect when I actually get there.

"I'm not sure. And not really," I admit. "But I have to at least try. There are innocent people, children, that are in danger."

"I would feel a little better if a couple of SWAT officers followed behind you," she says, almost pleading. On the message, it said that Amalia and I had to come alone, but technically we *would* still be alone if we got a five-minute head start on a SWAT van if it were to tail us. It's worth a shot.

"I would feel safer too. Maybe you can talk a few of them into it, but I have to go right now before it's too late. I love you, Mom." Now, tears stream down my face too.

"I love you too. I'll tell the SWAT captain where you're about to go and hopefully he'll agree to send a squad after you. You're so brave. You make me so proud," I give her another squeeze and then she turns around and disappears back into the door that she came out of.

"Finally ready?" Amalia asks me when I rejoin her.

"Born ready," I say. We both laugh because we know it's not true.

CHAPTER 9

F ive minutes later, Amalia sits in the passenger seat
next to me. She wears a jumbo, fur-lined jacket that
survived the fiery inferno to cover her bare arms
from the chilly weather. In the back seat, there is a bag of
weapons, which we quickly scooped up on the way back to
the car. Inside of the bag are two shotguns, a revolver, and
an extremely sharp pocketknife that we collected from the
wreckage in the parking lot. Having at least a little protection eases my nerves a bit. Hopefully, Mom will successfully
convince the SWAT captain to follow closely behind us, but
there is no time to stick around to see if they do. According
to the message, the killing will begin in thirty minutes. The
engine of the car roars to life and I step on the gas to leave
behind our sanctuary.

"So… about this weather," I say to break the ice after we
ride for five minutes in total silence. We haven't passed a
single car on the road in the short time that we've been away
from the hospital. I glance into the rearview mirror constantly, hoping that the SWAT captain agreed to Mom's request, but no headlights have come into view so far.

"You don't have to do that. We don't have to be friends,"
Amalia says as she stares out of the window at the trees as
they blur by. We've reached the stretch of road where the
deer was carried off into the forest earlier. I ease off the gas
a little just in case any more wild animals run out in front of
me, since the last thing we need is to get sidetracked again.

"I don't like awkward silence. Plus, we have to come up

with a plan for when we get there. Do we go in guns blazing or would stealth work better?" I ask her.

"How comfortable are you with using one of those? I've never shot a gun before in my life. They scare me," she says, jerking her thumb at the black bag that slides around in the back seat.

"I've never shot one either, but Sally the Red Cross nurse said the only way to kill those freaks is a bullet to the back of the head. It doesn't feel like they want to start a war though, they could've just attacked everyone at the hospital. This is different," I say as I make a right turn back into the residential neighborhood that we traveled through earlier. The road is still dark, with only a few streetlights that remain lit. Lightning suddenly flashes in the sky and comes as a reminder that tonight is far from over.

"Great. Blood might fall from the sky again. That's exactly what we need right now," Amalia says with a sigh as she slumps down in her seat and rests her head on the cold glass window. She shivers and rubs her hands up and down her bare legs. I crank up the heater. There's no way that the temperature is above forty degrees, which has to be some kind of record for the state of Texas. This is unheard of for the beginning of summer.

The dark silhouettes of the houses loom on both sides of the street, with most of the residents probably trapped back at the hospital since their cars were obliterated. The neighborhood takes no time to drive through and soon, I brake at a stop sign and the blue lights on top of the theater shine in the night sky directly in front of us.

Before I pull away from the stop sign, headlights appear in the rearview mirror. I breathe a sigh of relief. Mom has always been great at getting what she wants. Hell, I wouldn't be surprised if it's *her* driving a stolen SWAT van. I wait for the vehicle to drive a little closer before I get out of the car to talk to whoever's inside. Now that the vehicle is so close, I can tell that the bright lights are on too, not just the headlights.

"Stay here. Mom told me that she was going to convince the leader of the SWAT team to send a squad after us. I'm gonna go talk to the driver," I say, throwing the car into park as the headlights come to a stop in the rearview mirror. I have to shield my eyes from the blinding lights in order to see the driver.

With my hand cupped on my forehead like a sun visor, I only take one step before I freeze in my tracks. When the green driver's door opens, there is a white stripe that runs horizontally across it, not a SWAT logo plastered on the side. Instead of an officer in heavy tactical gear, out steps the deranged psychopath who murdered Jaden.

On this third encounter with the man, I'm convinced that his eyes permanently flit back and forth, which perfectly matches his crazed behavior. Luckily, my body doesn't go into shock so I'm able to fling open the back door of the car and search for the revolver in the oversized tote bag.

"What's going on?" Amalia asks, her voice filled with concern when she turns around and finds me rummaging through the bag.

"Stay in here. Don't move," I yell at her when she places one hand on the handle to open the passenger door.

"Are there more threaders?"

"No. The man who killed Jaden," I say as my hand connects with the cool, shiny metal of the silver gun. I also slip the foldable knife into my back pocket. Without another word to Amalia, I exit the car and reenter the cold night air more protected than ever.

The man moves slowly forward, away from the driver's door until he is bathed in the bright headlights of his SUV. I can no longer see his face or hands, which may hold a gun of his own, but only a silhouette of his figure.

"Don't take another step. I have a gun!" I scream, raising the heavy gun to point it at the shuffling shadow of a man. He listens to my order and doesn't move anymore. "Good. I want you to go back into your vehicle and turn off those damn headlights so I can see your face. You can move now. Slowly." He wordlessly obeys and when he steps out of the SUV to face me, his hands are above his head to show that he has no weapon.

"I'm not your enemy," he croaks in a voice that lacks the confidence of someone who ended a life hours earlier.

"I'll be the judge of that. Stop right there," I say when he's about ten feet away from me. I don't want him to get any closer, not until he coughs up some remotely believable information. "What is your name and who do you work for?" I ask, jabbing the gun toward his chest as an intimidation tactic. Honestly, I'm not even sure if this thing is properly loaded, but he doesn't need to know that.

He hesitates, looking anywhere but my face. "Elliot Hansen. I work for the A.M.E.D., a government organization. It stands for the Advanced Mutation of Epidemic Diseases. We keep track of...special diseases that could possibly affect a lot of people. We're like the World Health Organization, but more undercover." I find it hard to believe that this shaken up, nerve-ridden man is some kind of government official. I have to make sure that he's not lying before I lower my guard.

"Can I see some identification? A driver's license, a name badge from the government agency, anything like that," I demand.

"Yes. I'll reach slowly into my pocket to grab my wallet. Please put the gun down, I'm not going to hurt you," he says in a trembling voice. I leave the revolver in position, aimed right at where his heart is probably pounding rapidly in his chest. He lowers his right hand to remove the wallet from his back pocket and then walks forward to hand the bulky thing to me. I snatch it from his grasp when he gets close enough and then command him to get back into place a safe distance away from me.

His badge from the A.M.E.D. confirms the information that he fed me, with an emblem of three triangles arranged around the initials of the institution firmly stamped in the corner. I toss the wallet back to him, which he doesn't catch. It opens up when it hits the ground and I almost feel bad for him when money spills out and blows down the street in a cool gust of wind.

"Next question. Why did you run through the red light earlier and almost kill me? A government official should know better than that," I say, making sure that my voice reeks of sarcasm. I need to speed up this interrogation. Even though the theater is in sight and we still have twenty minutes before the threat in the message is set to begin, I would much rather be too early than too late.

"I was on my way to the theater. Yesterday, we received an anonymous tip that a biological attack was set to take place sometime today. The caller gave us an extensive list of potential targets, thousands of locations all over the entire country, and unfortunately, Royal Cinema was on there. The caller knew top-secret information and mentioned it in the tip so we knew it was a credible threat and not just some kid pulling a prank. We were warned that if we set off any red flags, such as trying to evacuate people from the list of targets, then more locations would be attacked. So, as a team, we decided that the best thing to do would be to send in agents undercover, posing as citizens, to diffuse any possible situations." He stops and his teeth chatter uncontrollably, from the chilling temperature or from nervousness, or maybe a mixture of both.

"We had to go about doing this in a careful, calculated way, so that whoever called in the threat wouldn't know that we were working against them. Undercover agents that already had assignments were reassigned to locations that we felt were in the most danger, which is how I ended up here in Briskwood. This was the only location in Texas on the list and because it's in close proximity to Houston, it set off a red flag for us. There's a team of A.M.E.D. employees in Houston right now and they were supposed to link up with me if any problems arose, but I haven't been able to get in touch with them for hours. We also work closely with the SWAT team." By the time he finishes, my head spins. This small city is the last place I would expect a biological terrorist attack to take place in. Maybe that's why they chose it.

"Okay," I say, only managing to get out the one word, trying to collect my thoughts from the tidal wave of new information. "So that's why you executed my coworker? Does A.M.E.D. not believe in quarantine?"

"Of course we do, but this was by far my biggest assignment yet and I flipped out under pressure. Now it's gonna cost me my job, if we even survive. This is not a good situation, Miles. No one predicted that the attack would come in the form of rain," he says, lowering his head. I almost mention that Jaden's life, or lack thereof now, was affected substantially more than his job, but I can tell that he's guilty about what he did.

"Why are you following me around? How did you even know where I went after I left to find my mom?"

"It's complicated, but you can make this right. I don't have the time to explain since you have to go to theater. I promise on my life that you will not be harmed, but—" He doesn't get the chance to finish.

Behind us, the quiet, unmoving neighborhood springs to life. Threaders erupt from the dark houses, propelling broken bricks, shards of shattered glass, and pieces of wood onto the slick street. The pack of leathery, gray creatures surge toward us at lightning speed. Some even run on all fours, bounding toward us like a pride of lions after a herd of gazelle.

I lower the gun from Elliot's chest and quickly back up, even though I could never even dream of moving fast enough to match the pace of the deadly creatures. Amalia peers around the back of the car at the wave of death, having emerged after the sonic boom of the houses being blown out ripped through the night.

I'm aware that this may be my last thought ever, but I can't help but notice just how perfectly uniformed they are, especially since there are so many of them. Threaders of all sizes make up the pack, but they all strongly resemble each other, with spikes that rise from everywhere on their muscular bodies and yellow eyes brighter than Elliot's blinding headlights. Elliot no longer faces me, but now looks to the incoming onslaught and for the time being, I forget any grudges that I have against the man.

When the first of them reach us, they don't immediately rip into us, but instead stop directly in front of Elliot. The heavy gun slips from my nervous hands and lands at my feet. Too terrified to lean down, I use my shoe to kick the weapon backwards, hoping that it slides far enough to reach Amalia on the other side of the car. First, she looks down to the ground and then nods at me to let me know that I was successful.

The threaders ignore Amalia and I and focus their full attention on Elliot, who is backed all the way up against the SUV. His nervous eyes no longer bounce from side to side, but remain fully open to stare at the maniacal creatures that appear to be amused by his obvious fear. A roar bellows from the center of the pack and I don't even have to look to know that it comes from the dreadful Pink Dress.

At the sound of the roar, the threaders closest to Elliot back away, but their deep, throaty laughter doesn't lessen. When they recede, the crowd opens up and I find Pink Dress directly in the middle, with an unconscious Salem cradled in her arms like a newborn baby. The only reason that I know she's alive is because of how she's positioned in the monster's arms, carefully placed to not be injured by any of the protruding spikes.

Pink Dress saunters toward Elliot like a celebrity on a red carpet, down a cleared path with her minions shoved off to the side vying for her attention. The hulking beast reeks of power that is evident in every slow, cautious step that makes it hard to believe that she is capable of moving at impossible speeds. When she reaches Elliot, she shifts Salem to one arm and uses the other to softly punch the man on his arm as if to tease him. He screams like a tow truck has hit him, which only intensifies the amusement of the threaders.

With a snicker of her own, Pink Dress walks away from the petrified man and goes to the back of the SUV to open the trunk. It must be locked because there is a little resistance when she tugs on it, but it doesn't last long under the immense pressure and after a few short seconds, it spins off down the street to join the debris from the destroyed houses. She lowers Salem into the open trunk and then returns back to the anxious, bloodthirsty crowd.

This time, she doesn't stop in front of Elliot, but much to my dismay, comes over to my car instead. Her hypnotizing yellow eyes jump back and forth between Amalia and I, as if she still hasn't made up her mind about what to do with us. After a few overwhelmingly tense seconds, she does what she does best (well, besides instill fear into the heart of everyone she encounters): utters a simple command.

"Go," she says to me, jabbing a pointed arm in the direction of the theater.

Before I can even react to the order, Elliot screams out. "MILES! DO NOT TRUST—" His voice catches in his throat.

Pink Dress moves so fast that it takes a few moments for my mind to register that she isn't in front of me anymore. Her arm is wrapped around Elliot's neck, squeezing the life from him like an anaconda.

"No!" I scream and jump toward the dying man, but the closest threaders surround me instantly and force me back to my car. I can only watch in horror as Elliot's mouth opens and closes as he tries desperately to inhale oxygen into his deprived lungs.

Finally, the life drains from his blue face, eyes frozen in place on the threaders that cheer to celebrate his death. Pink Dress removes her arm from his neck and allows his limp body to slump to the ground. Her supporters rally behind her as she leans down and uses one of the arm spikes to slice away Elliot shirt and reveal his unmoving chest to the cold night air. The next thing that she does tells me exactly why the news decided to give them the name 'threaders.'

First, she uses a spike to prod Elliot's bare chest, much like the poor doe with the broken leg. She then uses the spike to trace a vertical line down his chest and onto his stomach, opening him up like a surgeon at an operating table. Blood comes from everywhere and forms a large puddle on the concrete, soaking the bare feet of Pink Dress. The cacophony from the crowd of threaders explodes, so loud that I have to cup my hands over both of my ears and Amalia does the same. My legs refuse to move and I tell myself that it's because Elliot promised my safety. The truth is, I just want this to be over, one way or another and I think this is my body's way of giving up. I'm unable to pry my eyes away from the horrific scene, even with Amalia screaming at me that it's time to leave.

Next, Pink Dress sticks the spike back into his chest cavity and moves the arm in a circular patter until his heart is cut free. At this point, my stomach bubbles violently. When she picks up the small, pink heart, my mother's lasagna comes back up all over the street. With the heart firmly grasped in her gray hands, she throws it backwards over her shoulder like a bride doing a bouquet toss at a wedding. Her followers eagerly jump for it, bumping into each other as they fight over the organ.

Pink Dress kneels over the body, repositioning the surgical spike in the place where his heart was. The spike is no longer dry, but coated in a vibrant green slime that travels up and down, defying the laws of gravity. The disgusting goo forms into a solid ball and then travels down the spike for one last time before it disappears out of sight into Elliot's chest. When Pink Dress stands up, the ball of goo is gone and only strings of it drip from the glistening spike. She has just replaced his heart with whatever the hell that was.

Satisfied with the job, she goes back down to the ground and stitches his chest closed with some kind of white string that hangs from one of the smaller spikes on her arm. She threads the string across his open chest, sewing back and forth until the wound is sealed shut. She lifts her head and roars into the sky one last time to celebrate the new addition to her group.

"Miles, let's go!" Amalia yells again over the disturbing celebration, but my eyes remain fixated on the spot where Elliot's body lies.

"GOOO!" Pink Dress repeats to us, much louder this time, as if she was too caught up in performing Elliot's transformation to notice us still standing here. Although her voice is angry, I swear for a second that the human part of her surfaces and her eyes cry out for help. I snap out of my trance and jump back into the car. The last thing I see before I burn off down the street is Pink Dress putting Elliot back into the driver's seat and then sitting on the ground, most likely to wait for his transition to take place.

As I skid into the parking lot of the theater, I nearly vomit again, but there is nothing inside of my stomach so acid just burns my throat instead.

"We can't go in there. I don't want that to happen to me," Amalia says in a shaky voice that fully encompasses everything we just witnessed. Her face has lost much of its color and she looks like she's about to pass out.

"I know I should feel scared after what we just saw, but I don't. I saw something in Pink Dress' eyes before we left," I say.

"Who?" she interrupts.

"The leader. The... surgeon," I say with a shiver and roll of my eyes.

"Oh."

"That's what I've been calling her in my head. It's really not that hard to figure out. But anyway, I saw something in her eyes when she commanded us to leave, almost like she was pleading for us to get out of her face before she turned on us against her will." When I say this out loud, I realize that I should've just let it remain a thought in my head because it sounds crazy. It's just a gut feeling that I have.

"So you're the threader whisperer now?" Amalia snaps back. We don't have time for this. The clock on the radio reveals that we only have ten minutes to go before everyone will be murdered, or worse, murdered and then dissected like Elliot.

"Let's go," I say as I jump out of the car and lock it behind me.

"You're forgetting two things," she yells, but I don't stop walking.

"One! This." Something hard hits me on the back and I turn around to find the bag of weapons lying at my feet. When I look up at her, she has the revolver in one hand, having picked it up after I kicked it to her underneath the car. "And two. Salem is back there. With them." She waves the gun over her shoulder at where the threaders still sit on the ground, surrounding the SUV. I almost forgot that Salem, one of the main reasons that we're out here in the first place, got tossed into the back of the trunk before Elliot's murder.

"Look. I want to save her as much as you do, but we can't just waltz over there and snatch her without dying ourselves. Plus, there are tons of other people at risk too. She'll probably be brought inside with us once we go in there." I point a finger toward the blinking blue lights on top of the building. I wish there was a way to save both Salem and the customers, but it doesn't seem possible. I think of the innocent, helpless children from the Rodriguez family and know that going into the building is the right thing to do.

Amalia sighs, but doesn't start a fight because she probably knows that I'm right. This is our best, actually our *only* option. We would get annihilated if we went back over there to the threaders. I'm sure of it.

Before I scoop up the bag of weapons, I pull out a shotgun and load it up in what I think is the correct way. The shells click into place with a satisfying click, so I assume that's a good thing.

I glance over my shoulder at her. "Let's do this."

I press my face up against the glass door to the building and find no one in sight. All of the lights are on, which almost makes it seem like we're open, but the hustle and bustle of the lively business has been reduced down to absolutely nothing. Much to my surprise, the door opens when I pull on it. The doors are never open this late, but according to the picture on the watch, Mr. Vega was a little too tied up to lock the building.

"Hello! We're here," I scream in the open, empty lobby. My voice echoes down the corridors as I raise the gun and point it in front of me.

"Hi, Miles. Glad you could make it," a distorted voice says on the intercom system high above our heads. The voice sounds robotic and artificial, like some kind of device has been used in order to mask the person's (or threader's) true identity.

"I don't like this," Amalia says as she steps up closely behind me, her warm breath tickling my neck. Her knuckles have lost color from gripping the revolver so tightly.

"Look. You obviously have some kind of an issue with me, but those customers and Mr. Vega are innocent. Let them go." I shout up to the ceiling at the speaker where the voice came from. If someone outside passed by right now, I'm sure I would look ridiculous to them.

"Can't do that," the computerized voice replies. Suddenly, the lights go out for what feels like the millionth time today and a blanket of impenetrable darkness suffocates us.

"We need to stand back to back." I shout to Amalia. Since I'm so much taller than her, my butt ends up awkwardly placed on her back as we get into a defensive position. "Aim your gun in front of you. Let's walk back to the front door." We shuffle backwards through the lobby, which seems painfully large without being able to see where we're going.

"I wouldn't do that if I were you," the voice speaks again, sounding as amused as a robotic voice can. As I place my hand on the door so we can get the hell out of here until we come up with a better plan, the rumbling clouds above release a crimson waterfall that makes the rain that started all of this look like a harmless mist. The shower of death rain blows under the covered canopy and coats the glass door until we can no longer see out of it. We're trapped.

"Oh my God," Amalia whispers.

"Now that we're on the same page, please walk down the lit corridor so that we can begin." While the sudden torrential downpour distracted us, the creepy Big Brother voice must have turned on the lights to one of the hallways; the hallway where Jaden's blood is probably still fresh on the carpet.

"Put down those weapons. I made it perfectly clear that you would not be harmed. They won't do you any good anyway," the voice says as we blindly move through the lobby to the bright hallway.

"We might as well not piss this person off," I whisper to Amalia as I reluctantly place the shotgun on the tile floor. As I lean down, my back pocket shifts and I feel the pocket-knife still in place. I leave it exactly where it is and don't set it down next to the gun.

"I hope you know what you're doing," she whispers back and then places the gun down next to mine. We step into the hallway, leaving the abyss of a lobby behind. There is no sign of life in the hallway and no sign of Jaden's body either.

"Good. See you two in a few minutes." The lights go out once again and leave us stranded at the edge of the hallway, with only more blackness behind us in the lobby.

"Stop playing these games, man. Or woman. Or thread-er. Whoever the hell you are! Just tell us what—" Amalia snaps, shouting at the top of her lungs, but is promptly cut off. It's much too dark for me to see anything, but when she screams, it sounds muffled as if someone has a pillow firmly pressed over her face.

"Hey!" I scream, but someone grabs me from behind and places what feels like a towel or a blanket over my face. When the slightly sweet smell pours into my nose, it becomes more and more difficult for me to remain upright.

I kick my legs and try to free my arms, but the strength of whoever has a hold on me coupled with the chemicals that flood my brain renders my muscles useless. Finally, I stop fighting and let the darkness swallow me whole.

The first thing that I'm aware of when I awaken is that I can't breathe. I'm inside of the auditorium from the screen on the pocket watch, tied down with rope to one of the leather seats near the front. The dimly lit, giant screen that stretches from wall to wall is directly in front of me and provides the only source of light since the rest of the auditorium is dark.

A soft moan escapes from someone to my right and I turn my head to find Amalia two seats down from me, with rope wrapped around the thick jacket that she is still bundled in. "Amalia," I whisper to her in a voice that comes out strained and weak since the rope constricts my chest. She moans again and pivots her head to look at me, but I can't see her face because her long braids act as a veil that she can't move because of her restrained arms.

"Where are we?" she asks in a breathless voice that matches mine.

"In the auditorium from the picture on the watch." I've cleaned these auditoriums so much over the past few years that I can identify which one we're in just by looking at how the seats are arranged. We're inside of number four, the one where we found the dead birds outside of the exit door. We're on the third row and the two in front of us are empty. In the picture, it looked like Mr. Vega and the customers were at the top of the auditorium.

Because of the rope, I'm unable to turn around and see if anyone is in here with us. My neck is stiff by the time I stop twisting it, trying my hardest to search for any signs of life, but the farther away from the screen, the harder it gets to see anything at all in the pitch darkness.

"Hello," I weakly scream, but I doubt anyone can hear my pathetic attempt at a cry for help. I may not be able to use my voice, but there are other ways to make noise. Since this theater is super old, not much has been repaired in a long time, including the seats. Luckily, the one that I'm tied down to creaks loudly even from the slightest movement.

I rock back and forth, hoping that someone will finally acknowledge my presence. In this process of rocking back and forth, I remember that I still have the knife I found in the hospital's parking lot in my back pocket. With two fingers, I pinch the folded blade and carefully slide it out so that it doesn't fall to the sticky floor underneath me. I have already sliced through two of the many layers of rope by the time someone speaks.

"Is someone down there? It's pitch black up here, I can't see a thing," a male voice yells down.

"Yes. It's Miles," I reply and even though I have a long way to go before all of the rope is cut free, my voice already sounds stronger since I can breathe a little more.

"Miles!" It's Mr. Vega. He sounds excited when he realizes that it's me. "Is Trevor down there with you?"

"No, he's still back at the hospital. It's a long, long story. What is going on here?" I say as the fourth rope severs under the blade of the sharp pocketknife.

"When we were upstairs in the projection booth, someone knocked on the door and I thought the police had finally showed up. Before I even cracked the door open, I made the person speak so we wouldn't have a repeat of the last time. Everything seemed fine, the man said that he was a cop before I even mentioned that we were waiting for the police." A child cries out, which lets me know that Mr. Vega isn't alone up there, so the other hostages probably haven't been moved.

"Then, things went south. The man flashed me his badge through the crack in the door so I opened it, because why wouldn't you trust a cop, right?" His voice drips with sarcasm. "Anyway, when I opened it, he shot me with a stun gun, and the rest is history. No idea who did this to us or why."

"Who is up there with you?" More pieces of rope are under me, sliced in half, than are wrapped around me now. It's a lot easier to move and I would be able to answer my own question to Mr. Vega if only it weren't so dark in here.

"Cesar and Marisela Rodriguez with their two children, Ms. Suzanne and her sisters, Clementine and Rebecca, and myself. That's all."

"Has the voice spoken to you over the intercom?" I ask.

"No. We've sat here in the dark for hours, tied up and unable to do anything. Why are you back here anyway? I thought you went to find your mother." Before I can answer him, the voice on the intercom returns and interrupts our Q&A session.

"Welcome back to the world of the living, Miles and Amalia. So glad that you two could join our little party. Let's see those beautiful faces." The voice is still altered, but it sounds lighthearted and amused, as if all of this is a game. This makes me nervous. The worst villains are always the ones who find what they do amusing. I mean, just look at the Joker.

The bright white lights on the ceiling suddenly come back on and blind me. Tears stream down my face and I can't wipe them because my arms are stuck in place behind my back.

"Oh, and Miles, don't cut through those last ropes, or you'll regret it. I can promise you that much," the voice threatens. Damn it. I only had about five more to cut through before I was completely free. I have no idea how this person can even see what I'm doing because as far as I know," we don't have cameras inside of the auditoriums. I close the knife and shove it back into my pocket.

"You should have moved faster," Amalia says, shaking her head like a wet dog to move some of the braids from her face.

"It's harder than it looks. You must have forgotten that I'm being squeezed too," I shoot back.

"Are you two done so that we can begin?" the voice cuts in. Neither of us says a word. "I asked you two a question. I hate that I have to do this, but you've given me no choice. You will learn to follow simple instructions and commands eventually or people will die."

Behind me, there is a sharp pop and then someone cries out in pain.

"Oh my God, there's so much blood!" a woman yells, but I can't tell who it is.

"Mr. Vega! What's going on?" I yell, twisting around to look up at the other hostages.

Marisela, along with Ms. Suzanne and her sisters, and Mr. Vega, all stare at Cesar with horrified looks on their faces. The two children cry loudly, but their mother ignores them. Now that the lights are on, I can see everything in the auditorium.

Cesar has been shot. A red stain blossoms on the shoulder of his white shirt. His head lulls back and forth, like he's about to lose consciousness.

Marisela screams at him, but cannot do anything to help since she is tied up. "Cesar! Please stay with us! Listen to my voice!" She pleads desperately, her cries matching those of her children.

"Oh, don't be dramatic. He'll live. That was just a flesh wound, but next time I won't be so nice. And remember,

I have a perfect view of each and every one of you from up here in the projection booth. Now, it's time for the show to begin. Sit back, relax, and enjoy the presentation. Sorry, there's no popcorn," the voice says and the lights turn back off like how they do when a movie is about to begin.

Instead of a normal movie, a black and white video plays. It closely resembles a documentary or found footage film, not an actual movie. A tall barbed wire fence surrounds a small building with a single light bulb hanging over the entrance door. On the door, there is an insignia for the U.S. Army along with an American flag. Words appear that tell us that date: December 4, 1943. The camera pans out to reveal that the building is located in a remote, snowy location with no other man-made structures in sight.

The scene changes and goes to the inside of the building, which is actually some kind of makeshift laboratory that looks too advanced for the year 1943. The outside of the building made it look minuscule and abandoned, which may have been the point when it was built so it wouldn't attract a lot of attention. The lab is built inside of a large open space, like an airplane hangar or an old warehouse, and doctors in white lab coats run around like headless chickens to the different stations that are set up everywhere.

After giving an overhead view of the entire lab, we find out what is behind one of the curtains. A mob of doctors stand around a metal operating table in the center of the room, furiously copying down notes onto charts on their clipboards. A man that wears only a hospital gown is strapped down to the table, with strips of leather across his neck, torso, and legs to keep him from moving. A bag of dark red liquid, not unlike the blood rain, is connected to an IV and drips slowly into the man's arm. His screams are continuous and unfaltering, so loud that his throat must have turned raw after five minutes of yelling. A couple of the doctors wear earmuffs, while the ones unlucky enough not to have any cycle between slamming their hands over their ears and quickly scribbling on their clipboards.

"Increase the speed of the drip. Slightly," a doctor with flaming red hair says authoritatively to a nurse that stands at attention next to the IV machine. The doctor is tall and awkward looking, with bifocal glasses that are slightly too large for his thin face. The nurse adjusts the drip and more of the potent liquid spills out of the bag into the plastic line that runs into the man's arm.

The man's screaming intensifies and dark veins pop up all over his face. A vessel in his right eye bursts and causes a lake of blood to form around his pupil. The red haired doctor furrows his eyebrows and chews on the top of his pen in confusion. "There has been no change from three days ago. Stop the treatment. Damn it." He throws the clipboard down and storms out of the curtain, shoving several other doctors out of the way. The nurse turns off the IV and pulls the needle out of the man's arm, setting it down on a small metal table. His hellish screams stop and are instead replaced by soft whimpering. The prominent veins that threatened to pop off of his face go back to normal, sinking down into his sweaty skin.

The other doctors follow behind the red haired man, but the nurse hangs around for a few more seconds, pretending to organize surgical instruments. When the last doctor leaves out, she leans down to whisper into the exhausted man's ear. "I'm so sorry about all of this. I'm going to think of a way to get you out of here." She brushes her lips across the man's red cheek and then exits the room.

When the nurse leaves, the man's heart rate on the monitor drastically increases. At first, I think that it's just a response from receiving affection after what has probably been a torturous past few days, but after a few seconds, it becomes clear that something else is going on. The heart monitor flatlines and three of the doctors that just left out race back in, flinging open the curtain and revealing the rest of the medical stations where more horrible experiments are probably happening.

A female doctor turns off the monitor, stopping the piercing, monotonous beeping. The sound is replaced by silence, except for the grunts of a male doctor as he does compressions on the man's hairy chest.

"It's not working. Grab the paddles," he yells to the others. One of them runs over to the counter and grabs a portable defibrillator machine. The doctor removes his gloved hands from the unconscious man's chest to charge the paddles. After several failed attempts, he looks at the watch on his wrist and calls the time of death. The man's head falls to the side and pink foam pours out of his open mouth. The doctor rips off the gloves and tosses them down with an exasperated sigh.

The doctor with fiery red hair reenters the tent and demands to know what happened. He is obviously the boss and the others appear nervous when they try to explain, stammering and speaking over each other.

"One at a time," he says firmly and raises a freckled hand to silence them. "Thomas. Speak."

Thomas is the doctor who tried and failed to save the doomed man. The chubby doctor still stands next to the body, guilt plastered all over his face. "Well, I heard the heart monitor beeping so I ran in here to check it out. I was the first one to get in here, so I started compressions, and when that failed, I used the defibrillator. You know, standard stuff. It didn't work, so I called the time of death." He is visibly shaken and shows that he is not used to being put on the spot for something so important.

The boss is not impressed by the testimony. "Were you aware that this case was not 'standard stuff'?" he asks in a mocking voice.

"Yes, but—"

"Are you incompetent?" He walks over to the man and plucks him on the forehead. " I don't recall asking you for an explanation. I just needed to know if you were aware of the circumstances. Get out of my face." The doctor explodes, his personality matching the color of his flaming curly locks.

"Sir, I did every—"

"GO, NOW. BEFORE I MAKE YOU THE NEXT TEST SUBJECT!" When he yells, everyone in the room leaves out, as if they know his breaking point and that nothing they say right now will make him cool down.

The doctor looks down at the corpse and sighs deeply. He grabs some towels from the counter and dabs around the man's mouth, wiping the pink foam away from his stubbly beard. He drops the moist cloth to the ground and uses another to wipe the fresh sweat from his forehead, as if he is prepping him for a funeral.

After he is satisfied with the clean up job, he gently strokes the man's hair and whispers softly to him. "We were so close. I could feel it. We were on the verge of a magnificent breakthrough." He leans down and kisses his forehead. "Rest well. Your sacrifice will not be in vain."

He begins to walk away, but stops and a frown materializes on his face. He goes back to the body and sticks two fingers under the man's nostrils. "What the—"

A hand reaches up and grabs the doctor by his neck. The man sits up from the operating table, ripping away the leather straps like they are made of paper, with the doctor gripped in one hand.

He lifts the doctor off of his feet and jumps down from the metal table. His eyes are crazed, lacking the fear and helplessness that was present before. His mouth twists into a cruel smile. "Rest well. Your sacrifice will not be in vain," he says, repeating the doctor's own words to his terrified face.

He launches the doctor into the flimsy curtain, which instantly wraps around him when it rips free from the ground. Satisfied with his work, he walks over to look into the camera. His face is a cobweb of red veins and when his lips curl into a devilish smile, the screen fills with gray static.

CHAPTER 10

"Just beautiful, isn't it? The start of something new. Gives me chills every time," the voice says, clicking in on the intercom above us and gushing with emotion as the picture fades from the screen. The video totally drew me in and when the voice speaks, I nearly jump out of my seat, but the few remaining ropes hold me back.

"Didn't that liquid look like oddly similar to the tidal wave we almost walked into a few minutes ago?" Amalia whispers feverishly.

"Amalia, dear, it's not polite to whisper. Please speak up for all to hear. Or else." A gun is cocked directly into the microphone, a promise of more violence to come if we don't do exactly what this psychopath says.

Amalia clears her throat before she shouts up to the ceiling, "I SAID, THAT LIQUID LOOKS SIMILAR TO THE TIDAL WAVE MILES AND I ALMOST WALKED INTO." I can just picture her eyes beneath the braids, rolling into the back of her head in annoyance.

"That's much better. I think I owe you an explanation, but let's do it face to face. Be down there in a few minutes!" The intercom clicks off and a million ideas of how to escape instantly flood my mind. "Oh, and one more thing before we meet. Miles, if I come down and you're free, one person will be shot for every sliced rope."

Well, that puts a damper on like, ALL of my plans. Fantastic. I think to myself as I breathe out a frustrated puff of air.

"How's Mr. Rodriguez doing?" I yell behind me, nearly

forgetting about the man getting shot, until the cocking of the gun into the microphone served as an unwelcome reminder.

"He's holding on. Currently unconscious, but his breathing seems steady enough. We have to get him out of here immediately though," Mr. Vega shouts down. I can't even imagine how Mrs. Rodriguez feels right now, being so close to her injured husband, but unable to do anything to save him. I just hope the oldest son, who is probably well aware that something is wrong, isn't pestering her with questions about why his father is asleep.

"Miles," Amalia whispers to me again. She waits for me to turn in her direction before she continues. "I have a knife too."

"What? Where is it?" I ask, unable to keep the excitement from entering my voice.

"It's in my back pocket. If you distract this weirdo when he finally decides to grace us with his presence, I may be able to cut myself free. I just have to make sure I'm discreet about it and don't let the ropes slip down from my body." I look down at my chest at the messy tangle of bindings and realize that it's no wonder I was exposed when I tried to escape; I wasn't secretive about it at all.

"Are you sure that you can keep them from sliding down? This guy means business. I don't want anyone to die on our hands." This is not a good plan. I think our best bet is to figure out what the hell is going on first. Maybe it's something we can talk our way out of, but somehow, I doubt it.

"I was a Girl Scout. That has to count for something, right? I think I can do it," she says, sounding sure of herself.

"I don't feel good about this. Let's just hear this guy out before we do anything drastic." My stomach rumbles in agreement, empty after expelling the partially digested lasagna all over the street.

"Sure, whatever," she says unconvincingly, which makes me think that she's still going to try to free herself.

After a few minutes, when the owner of the mysterious voice still doesn't show up, my mind wanders back to the video. Since the black and white video was apparently recorded in 1943 and the man reacted similarly to Jaden when the red liquid entered his body, I'm going to go out on a limb and say that this attack has been planned for a long time. Although the man didn't seize out or grow spikes like Jaden, they both appeared to be dead and then showed otherwise a few minutes later. Plus, when he tossed the tall doctor aside like a rag doll, he revealed that he had super strength just like the threaders.

This was not a random video to intimidate and scare us, but it offered vital clues into what the entire situation means; the bagged liquid being pumped into the man's body, the charts, which probably contained a record of information for an extensive period of time. The rain is not a freak accident of nature; someone *meant* for all of this to happen. Elliot must have been telling the truth about everything.

I fill Amalia in on my theory just as the door loudly creaks open below us and the cleaning lights turn on. The tension is evident when the entire room falls silent as we anxiously wait for the maniac to make an appearance.

Whistling shatters the eerie silence, coming from the inclined plane that leads up to where we sit. The person bangs on the side of the staircase, which makes me jump again. I gulp and look over to Amalia. I only have seconds to make sure that we're on the same page about her disastrous idea. I need to know what she plans to do if she's able to successfully cut herself free and not get herself killed in the process.

"What are you gonna do?" I wordlessly say to her, making sure that nothing comes out of my mouth.

"I'm not sure yet," she whispers back and does her best attempt at a shoulder shrug under the tight ropes. I lean my head back against the seat and close my eyes. We're doomed.

"Amalia, you are going to get everyone in here killed!" I shout in a whisper, as the whistling grows ever louder and another fist pounds into the side of the staircase. I can't tell if the person has moved at all or if they stand in one place, playing mind games with us. "Think of the two children up there before you make your decision. Again, I strongly advise against it."

I'm still trying to convince her not to try anything when her eyes suddenly double in size, staring far over my shoulder. Before I even turn around, I know that the madman has entered the seating area.

When I see the two people who stand at the bottom of the staircase, I actually have to blink my eyes more than a few times to make sure I'm not trapped in some terrible nightmare, unable to awaken myself with a pinch because of my restricted arms.

My grandfather, Ezekiel Walton, stands there in all of his six-foot tall, cancer-free glory, whistling a tune. My grandfather, who works on a military base in south Texas, here in Briskwood. My grandfather, who purchased me a brand new car last year. It catches me so off guard that I don't even realize that this revelation isn't even the most shocking part. When he steps aside, my jaw falls to the ground.

"That's him!" Mr. Vega exclaims from behind me. "That's the man who shot me with the stun gun!"

Behind him is Mr. Panderson, alive and well, decked out from head to toe in a police uniform.

I'm not sure if it's because of how familiar I am with these two people or what, but every ounce of fear in my body evaporates and is replaced by curiosity and confusion. Mr. Panderson and my grandfather, smiling up at us, and carrying the two shotguns that I recognize as the ones I found at the hospital. So many unanswered questions and things that don't add up in this twisted, weird situation.

"Grandpa?" I manage to choke out.

"Dad?" Amalia says at the exact same time.

"What did you just say?" I pry my eyes off of the strange scene at the bottom of the staircase and turn to make sure I heard her correctly. I'm not sure which of the two men she is talking about, but I pray it's not my grandfather.

"Dad," she repeats, "That is my father down there, in the police uniform. We don't see each other that often because I moved with my mom to New Orleans when they got a divorce a few years ago, but that's him." I look back and forth between my English teacher and her, not really seeing any resemblance between the two of them. He is a few shades darker than her and considerably heavier, balancing a balloon-inflated belly on top of two stumpy legs. I don't remember him even mentioning that he had a daughter in class, but he wasn't one to delve deeply into his personal life. If Mr. Panderson is truly her father, then now I know without a doubt where she gets her attitude from.

"Miles! Are you not going to say hello to your grandfather? Don't forget who bought you that fancy car you get to speed around in," Grandpa says as he ascends the stairs slowly, making his way to where we sit on the third row, and stopping Amalia from asking me any questions of her own. Mr. Panderson remains frozen in place, not even acknowledging his daughter's presence like a robot waiting to be activated.

"Grandpa... what is this?" I ask as he takes a seat next to me and wraps a surprisingly muscled arm around me in an awkward half hug. I shrug him off the best I can without the use of my arms.

"Why the cold shoulder? I've missed my grandson. It's been over a year since the last time we saw each other." I don't recognize the slimy, sarcastic man that sits in front of me. He's a bad impostor of the grandfather I know, who is always kind and willing to do anything for me. My grandfather would never carry a weapon around, much less use it to wound a father in front of his children and tote it around in front of his grandson.

"What is going on here?" I ask more sternly this time, showing that I am in no mood to have a family reunion. I wonder if Amalia still wants to cut herself free or if her father's appearance has her as shaken up as I am.

"First things first, I think you have something that belongs to us. Where is the golden pocket watch?" he asks, fumbling with something inside of his expensive suit jacket. He pulls out a small panel, with nothing on it but a red button directly in the center. It reminds me of the device in cartoons that controls nuclear missiles. It has a glass cover over it, most likely so he doesn't accidentally press it at the wrong time.

"I left it in my car. You didn't mention that I was supposed to bring it in here with me. I probably would have it with me if it didn't almost burn my friend's leg off," I spit back venomously.

"Shame." He flips open the cover and presses the intimidating red button. "Your car will be on fire shortly. I can give, but I can also take away." He smiles like he has done me a huge favor instead of just destroyed my most prized possession.

"Sorry about your watch, Henry. I had to overheat and destroy it since Miles forgot to bring it to us," Grandpa shouts down to Mr. Panderson, who just shrugs his shoulders and doesn't say a word.

Henry Panderson. The initials that were on the back of the watch were H.P. I never even thought of the teacher when I traced my fingers over the engraving. I wonder if it had some kind of tracking device in it and that's why we were easy to find at the hospital.

"What the hell is wrong with you? You just wasted your own money, you know, since YOU bought me that car," I shout, growing aggravated by this man's games. I need to know exactly what is going on right now.

"Settle down. I'll get you another one if this conversation turns out the way I want it to. We're special, Miles." He drops the disturbing, amused-by-everything persona and switches gears into business mode.

"What are you talking about?"

"The video that I just showed you. It was a project created by your great grandfather, my father, Samuel Walton. His goal in life was to create an indestructible, powerful new race of people. In a way, he achieved just that." He doesn't say, but I'm sure that my great grandfather was the head doctor, the one who got tossed aside by his own creation. It would explain where my full head of red hair came from since no one else in my family has it.

"What you saw was the first successful experiment on a

man named William Bronson. After the camera cut off, he became enraged at what he had become and murdered everyone inside of the facility, including my father. Shortly afterwards, he disappeared into the Rocky Mountains and was never heard from again, presumed to have died from a reaction to the treatment he received." I've never given any thought to Grandpa's father and he was never mentioned before. Now I know why.

"The liquid that you saw inside of the bag was a formula, Blood X, created by my genius father to enhance its recipients and is the same substance that has fallen from the clouds all over the country. I bet you're wondering how this is possible." He stops and waits for me to appear interested in this madness, but I just glare at him instead. He clears his throat and continues.

"Well, let's start with how I even got involved with this in the first place. My father knew that his work was dangerous and could possibly cost him his life, but he didn't care. This was for the greater good of all humanity and he was willing to be a martyr for his cause. Because of this, he kept a second record of all of his research and gave it to my mother for her to continue working on in the instance of his passing. He kept the record updated, all the way up to the day he died, and my mother had a lot of useful information to continue his dream."

"My mother believed her late husband to be insane and locked his magnificent work in a closet where it remained until she died. I was thirty years old when I stumbled upon the information. I had only been married to your grandmother, who has no knowledge of any of this might I add, for a short time and your mother was just a baby. I was so intrigued that I decided to continue his research and make our dreams one and the same," he continues, dabbing at his sweaty forehead with a towel.

"I don't understand. How were you able to get the formula from dripping inside of an IV bag to swirling around inside of a thunderstorm?" I ask, genuinely interested and in disbelief that I know the person behind the grotesque creatures running around terrorizing everything outside.

He holds up a hand to silence me and for a moment, I see his father in him. The mad doctor used the same gesture to interrupt his companions in the video. "You're jumping ahead. I decided that in order to move forward with creating a more efficient race of people, I would have to snake my way to the top and gain as much power as I possibly could. So, that's exactly what I did. Unspeakable acts have been committed in order for us to be sitting here today, talking about this master plan. I won't go into any details, but believe me when I say that they were one hundred percent necessary. The sacrifices that I made will all be worth it in the end."

I watch the words come out of his mouth and can't believe just how little I actually knew about him. This is a new person, the suppressed lunatic inside of him finally unveiled by his life's aspiration. I hope Amalia frees herself and is somehow able to overpower this stranger that spews nonsense in my face. I certainly won't get in the way if she wants to harm him.

"Let's fast forward to the present. At the top-secret facility in South Padre Island, myself, along with a team of excellent scientists, have created a way to generate thunderstorms with whatever we decide put in them. The devices, which have a compartment for my father's liquid of life, have to be placed into a body of water and then activated. What follows is a deviation of the water cycle and the results are the beautiful thunder showers that you've witnessed to-day. I decided to include Briskwood in my demonstration so you, Miles, could get an up close look at the future," he beams, proud of his wickedness. A wave of guilt washes over me when I realize that this whole day was a result of Grandpa wanting to give me an inside look into his experiment.

This seems so far fetched, but I can't argue that it's impossible since my English teacher who died this morning stands there watching all of this get explained to me. I hope he explains that part of it next. "This is insane," I whisper.

"Not insane, but revolutionary. Before I go into detail about the capabilities of this new race, I have two things to say. First, the creatures that you see running around wreaking havoc are not the final product, but just a prototype. A test of sorts, which is why the rain has only fallen over a few cities instead of the entire country. We still have a few kinks to work out, like those pesky spikes and horrible yellow eyes. I know they can be a little hard to look at, but they'll be just a figment of your imagination when all of this is over."

"Secondly, I may be putting my own head on the chopping block by telling you this, but there is an antidote and it's all around you. If you decide to not join in with me and become my enemy, I've given you a little head start," he laughs loudly, as if I would even consider not joining in with him to alter the course of humanity. If he's the one who tipped off Elliot's agency about the attack, then he's already revealed one flaw: cockiness. I can tell that he's overly confident because of the way he just blurts out that there's already an antidote.

I laugh along with him to hide the fact that I don't have any plans to join in with him. "Keep going. I'm intrigued."

I hope Amalia doesn't think I'm telling the truth and attacks me along with my grandfather if she gets free.

"I knew you would be! It's in our blood. Anyway, I know you must be dying to know how your teacher that you saw die is actually perfectly fine," he says, turning his attention away from me and to the motionless Mr. Panderson. I use the split second that his focus is on someone else to turn to Amalia and give her a look to let her know that I'm still on her side.

"I met Henry about five years ago, actually here in town when I came to visit. I saw him as the perfect candidate for my vision. He showed strong will and passion, so I secretly recruited him for my project. Every time he went away on a 'teacher's conference,' he came to visit me in South Padre and get an update on any breakthroughs that my team may have run across. Also, it's one hell of a coincidence that Amalia happened to come to the movies today. I just couldn't resist the opportunity for you two to learn about all of this together, so that's why I only requested the two of you to come. I had to use the customers and the triplet as bait." Salem. I hope she's still okay out there on her own, but if Grandpa is in control, then I hope he hasn't had a reason to eliminate her.

Amalia stares down at her father with a look of horror, having finally removed the braids from her face. "Dad, how could you do this? Do you know what happened to Granny Alice?" she shouts at him, tears streaking down her face.

"Don't waste your breath. He only answers to me now," he snaps at her.

"Get the knife." I hope she can read my lips through her watery eyes. My back is turned to Grandpa so hopefully he wasn't able to see what I just said.

"I mentioned how we still had to work out a few kinks with the formula. Actually, we have already done that, just not on a large scale. The new formula was given to Mr. Panderson last month when he volunteered to be our guinea pig." Last month, Mr. Panderson was out for a few weeks because of a surgery. When he came back, he was different, even more standoffish than before. The concoction circulating through his veins must have been the cause of his personality change.

"Today in class, you saw the most developed version of Blood X at work. I triggered the thunder that knocked out the power in the classroom, but held off on adding the formula to the device until later. This allowed Mr. Panderson to slow his heartbeat in the dark until it felt nonexistent. When you and your friend left to find help, he awakened and wiped the memories of all of the students, which is just one of the many special abilities that people receive under the influence of the formula. He is also incredibly strong." This explains why Sandra couldn't recall anything that happened in the classroom. It's all starting to come together now.

"When you returned to the classroom to find that the dead teacher and everyone else weren't there anymore, it made you look a little insane and therefore, anything you said for the rest of the day probably wouldn't be taken seriously. It cleared the path for me to roll out my plan smoothly." He claps his hands together suddenly, turning his attention away from me once again.

"Now, who wants to see a demonstration?" He spoke loudly enough for everyone in the auditorium to hear when he explained everything to me, so the others should be caught up on this unnatural turn of events.

"I do!" I say enthusiastically, remembering his threat to follow instructions from earlier. After all of this information that he disclosed, I'm not sure what he's capable of and I don't want to take any chances.

"Henry, bring your daughter to you. Just like we practiced." Mr. Panderson's eyes spring to life, no longer robotic and cold.

"Sure thing, Zeke. Come here, 'Malia and give me a hug," the English teacher shouts. With a flick of his wrist, Amalia rises, the ropes slipping over the top of her seat as she ascends into the air.

"Ah, telekinesis!" Grandpa exclaims, clapping his hands together like a five year old in a toy store.

Amalia screams, unable to control her body as she levitates through the air and comes to a halt on the bottom stair next to her father. He embraces her in a tight hug, but doesn't use his super strength since she remains in one piece. She tries to break away from his grasp, kicking and punching him, but he is unaffected by her attempts. After the hug, Mr. Panderson forces her back down the floor.

"Now, clear her thoughts. Put her at ease." Mr. Panderson obeys Grandpa mindlessly and it makes me worry about what he could force people to do if he somehow rolled out this version of the Blood X on a mass scale. I think he cares more about expanding his power than creating a race of people to make humanity better.

Mr. Panderson places his hands on the side of his daughter's head, who tries one last time to break away, but then goes limp. A few seconds later, she looks around in total confusion. "Where am I? Dad, what's going on?"

Grandpa smiles, impressed by his own creation. "This is only the tip of the iceberg. See what you could be a part of?

All you have to do is say the word and you're in," he smiles at me, waiting for me to accept his invitation. I have to pretend to agree with him because if not, then who knows what he'll do? I remember the other hostages in here, none of which have said a word since the big reveal. I wonder how Mr. Rodriguez is doing. We need to wrap this up so he can get some help.

"I've never seen anything like this before. I would be a fool not to be a part of something that could potentially change the course of history. Of course I'm in," I say and his face lights up, happy with my decision. "Does my mom know anything about this?"

"God, no. Can you imagine the lecture I would get?" He lets out a booming laugh. "Granny Catherine doesn't know about it either and she lives in the same house as me! She thinks I came up here to help you out with graduation activities."

"I only have one request. I'll go with you, but we need to leave right now and get Mr. Rodriguez some medical assistance. He's been nothing but kind to me and I don't want him to die. The other hostages can't be injured either," I demand.

"Of course, of course! The hostages have served their purpose and will not be harmed. Maybe I can even administer a small dosage of Blood X to help speed up his healing process," He reaches into my back pocket, pulls out the pocketknife, and then slices the rest of the ropes to free me from the chair. "Wait here while I free the others." I shoot daggers at the back of his head when he dashes up the stairs to where the hostages are. I'm so disgusted when I think of the blood on his hands. Jaden, Amalia's grandmother, Elliot who was an ally, not an enemy, and probably countless more people in the other cities where the blood rain fell.

He returns a couple minutes later with the hostages in tow behind him. Mr. Rodriguez is groggy, but alert and leans on his wife along with Mr. Vega for support. The two little boys travel down the stairs together, with the oldest holding little Julio's hand so he doesn't fall. Ms. Suzanne and her sisters bring up the rear, not moving any faster than when they held up the line in the projection booth.

When we get to the bottom of the staircase, Grandpa asks for everyone to stop before we leave out of the auditorium. "I know most of you have not been outside since all of this began, but I must let you know that the world has changed. It may appear to be more dangerous at first, but if any of my creations approach you, do not try to fight against them. You will not win. Succumb to their advances and they will make you one of them, more powerful than you have ever been. It's only up from here, folks," he says to the terrified group of people. I can't help but notice that he is dressed in all white, like some kind of religious cult leader. I have to turn my face to hide a scowl that I feel coming on.

"This isn't helping humanity. It's destroying it," Mr. Vega says angrily to my grandfather, shaking like a leaf. He's been quiet this whole time, but just from taking a glance at him, I know he's ready to explode.

"Humanity as it is right now is a disease, plagued with greed and sin. It's time for something new and I have taken it upon myself to bring about that change. No more waiting around," Grandpa says firmly. This man is absolutely insane. He preaches about bringing good will, but takes innocent people as hostages and has caused a ridiculous amount of secondhand damage.

"Go to hell," Mr. Vega spits back.

Grandpa raises the shotgun, which he still carries, and aims it at the manager. Everyone dives to the floor, except for Mr. Rodriguez, who is barely conscious and has the reflexes of a slug. "You'd better be glad I promised my grandson that I wouldn't harm any of you. Otherwise, this would play out a little bit differently." He lowers the deadly weapon.

I make eye contact with Amalia, who stares at me blankly as if she has no idea who I am. Before I can say anything, she stands up to face her father. "Dad, I'm scared and confused. Let's go home." I wonder just how much of her memory has been wiped since she hasn't lived here in Briskwood for years. She opens her arms and wraps them around him.

Mr. Panderson grunts and opens his mouth widely, like he's about to sneeze. Instead, a waterfall of blood pours out and drenches his faux police uniform. Amalia releases him from the hug and she's wild-eyed, wired. "You put your hands on my mother and I will not let you do the same thing to me," she says, revealing that the memory wipe did not affect her and that she's only been acting like it has.

He shoves her off of him and she flies through the air, smacking into the wall about fifteen feet away. She's unconscious before she hits the ground. When Mr. Panderson spins around, the knife that Amalia was going to use to cut herself free is embedded deeply into his flabby back, with only the hilt showing.

Mr. Panderson takes one look at my grandfather before he runs full speed toward the exit door. When he reaches it, he doesn't stop to use the handle, but instead uses his leg to kick it. He appears to be mostly unaffected by the blade and only the bloody saliva shows that he has been injured.

The door caves in and flies out into the night, no match for the power behind the kick. He glances over his shoulder once and then disappears into the night. The hole in the door acts as a funnel for the downpour of blood rain and the wind blows it inside, showering the screen with red specks. A cloud of liquid travels toward us and will cover the entire auditorium quickly if the rain keeps coming down at the rate that it is now.

"We need to get out of here. Now!" Grandpa yells. It seems that he is only confident in his precious Blood X when it's nowhere near his own skin. The fact that he is the first one to sprint out of the auditorium isn't a great selling point for the people he was just trying to promote his product to.

I tell everyone to leave ahead of me before I go to where Amalia is crumpled on the floor. I kneel down and shake her, fully aware that the cloud of death surges toward us. She groans and her eyes flicker open, but I don't have time for her to awaken completely. I hoist her up, balancing her on my shoulder just like how she did for me after Elliot shot Jaden. We exit the auditorium and slam the door shut behind us.

The scene in the hallway nearly causes me to drop Amalia back to the floor. People in HAZMAT suits are everywhere, some with guns and others with flashlights. "Get on the ground!" Someone blinds me with a flashlight as I fall to my knees and pull Amalia down with me.

On some of the suits, A.M.E.D. is written across the chest and on others, SWAT is written. "Are you Miles Parker?" A female SWAT officer asks. When I look around, I realize that none of the hostages are around and that Grandpa is the only one on the floor. I shield my eyes from the flashlight and stare up at the infuriated officer.

"Yes," I answer in a small voice, scared by all of the high-powered weapons pointed in my direction.

"Come with me," she says, lowering her weapon. Since Grandpa is the only one that remains on the floor with guns aimed at him, I can only assume that his plan backfired terribly and he's been caught. I hesitate for a moment, looking back and forth between him and the officer.

"You said you were with me, Miles. Don't let them take me. Let's just say this was a big misunderstanding and that there has to be another explanation. After all, my memory has faded a little. Sometimes I forget to lock the door when I leave home. How could I have possibly created a machine that turns the rain red?" He chuckles nervously and flashes me an ugly grin, pleading for me to go down with him. Now that he no longer has the upper hand, I don't have to act like his insanity holds any value to me.

"Old man, you're batshit crazy. I never want to see you again. It's time to go and clean up this mess you've made." I laugh in his face and walk away, dragging the groggy Amalia along with me.

"You'll regret this. This is only the beginning. I have more tricks up my sleeve," he growls behind me. I don't even turn around, but raise my middle finger into the air where I'm sure he can see it.

"Who is she?" The officer who asked my name helps Amalia and I walk through the mass of HAZMAT suits. She hands us two HAZMAT suits of our own and helps us squeeze into them, which makes us blend in with the rest of the crowd. This officer must be the captain because when we move through the crowd, she gives an order for the others to surround Grandpa and arrest him.

"Her name is Amalia. She's a friend," I say, deciding to leave Mr. Panderson out of this. Amalia is in no condition to answer a slew of questions about her father at the moment.

"Okay. I'm Captain Harriet Goldstein from the SWAT team. Your mother told us that you made the dumb choice to come out here with all of this mess going on." I knew Mom wouldn't take no for an answer when it came to sending a team to follow behind me. When I told her what I had to do, she probably made it her life goal to keep me safe.

Commander Goldstein continues. "But, she did explain the conditions and I have to say, it was an incredibly heroic thing to do. You saved all of those hostages, who are now being examined in a medical station we set up on the other side of the building. I didn't want to come after you with a team, but the group that we're working with, the A.M.E.D., tracked one of their people to a location very close to here and we had to check it out. Did you happen to see a man named Elliot Hansen anywhere around here?"

I gulp. "On the way here, did you see a large group of those threader things gathered around an SUV?" It's odd that they didn't recognize his green vehicle, but maybe he was so wired that he forgot to give them the information when he got to Briskwood.

"As a matter of fact, we did. We actually rescued the girl you came out here to save. She's in the lobby with her other siblings, along with your mother and friend Trevor." An elephant lifts from my shoulders when I learn that they're safe. I'm especially happy for Salem because I thought she was a goner.

"I'm so glad to hear that, but I have some bad news. What happened to the group of threaders down the street?" I ask.

"Well, when we drove up on them, I think we interrupted something big. They attacked us, so we had no choice but to use deadly force. A lot of them were killed, but a few got away. Why?"

"Because it's possible that Elliot was accidentally killed."

"Why do you say that?" She asks, frowning beneath the protective covering on her face.

"We met Elliot before we came in here. The threaders cut his heart out and replaced it with some green, gooey stuff. I assumed it was their way of turning him into one of them. If you didn't see his body, then he could've already turned and mixed in with the others that you shot at," I say. It took Jaden a while to grow the spikes, but his heart wasn't ripped out and replaced. Maybe Elliot's transformation would've taken less time since the substance pumped directly into his veins.

"I'll pass the information along to the commander of the A.M.E.D. You can go and see your people in the lobby now if you want. I'll be over there to ask you and Amalia some more questions in a little while." She releases Amalia and the full weight of the girl passes back to me, which will slow me down when we head back to the lobby.

"How did you know that my grandfather was the cause of all of this?" I ask as she starts to walk back to her officers that surround the old man on the floor. I have to know, just in case Mom bombards me with a million questions if she hasn't been informed that her father basically caused the apocalypse.

"According to the A.M.E.D., they've kept a close watch on him for a few months. In South Padre Island where this whole thing was orchestrated, there were several reports of strange weather events along with mutated animals. This put the facility that he worked at high on the list of potential causes. A.M.E.D agents were sent in undercover, but the project was so top secret that even they couldn't get access to any information about it. When he called in the tip about the attack, we were unable to trace the call to locate him. The moment we heard that there were hostages here, we knew he probably had something to do with it," she says and I have a hard time wrapping my mind around her words. Never in a million years did I see this coming.

I thank her for telling me the information and drag Amalia down the hall. She's mostly conscious now, mumbling under her breath every few seconds. I stop and shake her until she is fully aware of her surroundings because I can't walk another step without knowing why she attacked her father when he could've easily killed her. "Why did you do it?"

"I knew he probably wouldn't die from it, but I just couldn't control myself. My anger for him has been growing for a long time now and I finally snapped. The things he put my mom and I through..." She chokes up and I lay a supportive hand on her shoulder, totally understanding what it means to have a father that's hard to get along with. She looks down at my hand on her shoulder and starts to say something, but someone clears their throat next to us.

I didn't realize how close we had gotten to the lobby, but we have arrived at our destination where our friends and family wait for us. Emergency lights have been set up around the entire foyer, providing some relief from the darkness since the power is still out from when Grandpa turned it off and drugged us.

I take my hand off of Amalia's shoulder and awkwardly stare at the floor when Spencer, who wears a HAZMAT suit with no initials on the chest, looks less than impressed to see me with my hand on his girlfriend. For a second, I think he's about to say something, but when Amalia runs from my side and jumps into his arms, his face fills with joy. When they break away from each other, she hugs Scarlett and Salem too. Once they catch up, I have to go over and talk to Salem about her ordeal. I'm sure it's a great story.

I look behind them and find Mom talking with Trevor, their HAZMAT clad backs turned away from me. I tap both of them on the shoulder and am met with the tightest double bear hug that I've ever felt in my life.

"Miles! I would give you the biggest kiss right now, but we aren't allowed to take these hot suits off," Mom says, her breath clouding up the plastic on her suit.

"I'm so glad to see you, Mom. Thanks so much for sending the SWAT team after me. I don't know what I would've done without them. It's been a wild day." Now that the adrenaline has stopped pumping through my veins, I realize that I'm exhausted. It must nearly be dawn now and all of this started hours ago, when I went into work expecting it to be a normal night. I've never been so wrong about something in my life.

"At least we're all here together. It could've ended much worse," she sighs.

"Mom, did they tell you what started all—" I'm dying to find out if she knows about what Grandpa did, but she interrupts me with a shake of her head.

"Yes. We'll discuss it later. Talk to your best friend now." She gives me a sad smile and walks through the dark lobby toward the glass doors at the front. Amalia and the triplets join us in the center of the lobby, almost at the same spot where all of the rescued customers met up at earlier.

"Miles, I just have to say, thank you so much for coming after me. It means a lot," Salem says and gives me a hug. She looks virtually the same, but her red glasses are missing and her face looks empty without them.

"It's no problem. I wish I could've done more to help, but Amalia and I were severely outnumbered," I say, suddenly feeling bad because I was willing to sacrifice her to save the others.

"It's the thought that counts. If the script was flipped and Spencer was requested to come after me, he would probably already be back in New Orleans," she says, turning on her brother. Spencer shouts at her in response and they begin to argue, their favorite thing to do. Scarlett jumps in to defend her sister and they break away from us, lost in their yelling match.

"So, did you kick some threader ass?" When Trevor asks me this, I realize that I didn't even use the weapons I collected once. They were more of a prop than anything else. Since the threaders never seem to travel alone, two shotguns and a revolver were useless against the powerful pack.

"Not exactly. But Amalia did kick her father's, who happens to be Mr. Panderson by the way," I say in a nonchalant way just to see his reaction. Amalia and I collapse into a fit of laughter. The look on his face is priceless, with his mouth hanging agape.

"WHAT? HE'S ALIVE? AND HE'S HER FATHER? WHAT?" he screams the series of questions, which makes us laugh even harder. Before I can gain control of my laughter, Mom calls for us to come over to where she stands looking out of the glass.

She has the door slightly cracked open, enough so that freezing air from outside blows in. The glass is still streaked from when the whirlwind of Blood X covered it, but through the open door it is clear what she wants us to see.

I push past her and go outside to get a better look, figuring that the HAZMAT suit will offer protection from the phenomenon that lies before me.

A layer of snow has accumulated on the ground. If that isn't weird enough for the middle of May, it's not fluffy and white like regular snow.

It's pink.

ACKNOWLEDGMENTS

It all started with a raindrop behind a movie theater. So first, I would like to thank my parents, Angelique and Willie Joubert, for HIGHLY suggesting that I apply at Cinemark Tinseltown for my first job. This story might not exist had I not taken their advice.

My cousin and editor, Rylee Babino —the only person brave enough to read through this rollercoaster of a story not once, but TWICE! Thank you for being so supportive and convincing me that this story was worth sharing with the world. I can't wait to read your New York Times best sellers when they come out in the future.

My second editor, Devan Cramer — thank you for reading through my novel and offering suggestions, as well as sharing your own work with me. I feel that I gained a vast amount of knowledge from reading your pieces.

My sister, Christiana Joubert — thank you for being the best sister I could ever ask for. You have not only been supportive of this project, but for every aspect of my life. Also, thank you for only being slightly annoyed while taking my author photo. I know I'm a hard model to work with.

My friends, Janell Chaney and Mercedes Celestain — thank you both for supplying comic relief in times of stress!

My friend, Jess Rigsby — thank you for never judging me and being a beacon of light in my life.

My grandmothers, Delores Babino and Jessie Joubert — thank you for always being like second mothers to me and of course, for the amazing meals you both provide.

Lastly, I would like to thank my grandfathers, Willie Roy Joubert Sr. and Joseph "Sonny" Babino, who unfortunately are not here to see my first novel come out.